The Hidden Worlds

The Hidden Worlds

Sandra Ingerman

&

Katherine Wood

MOON
BOOKS

Winchester, UK
Washington, USA

First published by Moon Books, 2018
Moon Books is an imprint of John Hunt Publishing Ltd., No. 3 East Street, Alresford
Hampshire SO24 9EE, UK
office1@jhpbooks.net
www.johnhuntpublishing.com
www.moon-books.net

For distributor details and how to order please visit the 'Ordering' section on our website.

Text copyright: Sandra Ingerman and Katherine Wood 2017

ISBN: 978 1 78535 820 3
978 1 78535 821 0 (ebook)
Library of Congress Control Number: 2017952288

A CIP catalogue record for this book is available from the British Library.

Design: Stuart Davies

Printed and bound by CPI Group (UK) Ltd, Croydon, CR0 4YY, UK

We operate a distinctive and ethical publishing philosophy in
all areas of our business, from our global network of authors to
production and worldwide distribution.

Contents

This book is dedicated to Jordan, Carter, Grant and Gavin, and their Power Animals, Chee, Yani, Bear and Dali, and all of the young people of the world. May your spiritual practices and your power animals help you create a joyful and meaningful experience that helps all of life and the Earth.

Books/Audio Programs/Transmutation App all by Sandra Ingerman

Soul Retrieval: Mending the Fragmented Self
(HarperOne 1991)

Welcome Home: Following Your Soul's Journey Home
(HarperOne 1993)

A Fall to Grace (fiction)
(Moon Tree Rising Productions 1997)

Medicine for the Earth: How to Transform Personal and Environmental Toxins
(Three Rivers Press 2001)

Shamanic Journeying: A Beginner's Guide, book and drumming CD
(Sounds True 2004)

How to Heal Toxic Thoughts: Simple Tools for Personal Transformation
(Sterling 2007)

Awakening to the Spirit World: The Shamanic Path of Direct Revelation, book and drumming CD
(co-written with Hank Wesselman)

The Shaman's Toolkit: Ancient Tools for Shaping the Life and World You Want to Live In
(Weiser 2010)

Walking in Light: The Everyday Empowerment of a Shamanic Life
(Sounds True 2014)

Speaking with Nature: Awakening to the Deep Wisdom of the Earth
(co-written with Llyn Roberts)
(Inner Traditions 2015)

Audio Programs

The Soul Retrieval Journey
(Sounds True 1997)

The Beginner's Guide to Shamanic Journeying
(Sounds True 2003)

Miracles for the Earth
(Sounds True 2004)

Shamanic Meditations: Guided Journeys for Insight, Vision, and Healing
(Sounds True 2010)

Soul Journeys: Music for Shamanic Practice
(Sounds True 2010)

Shamanic Visioning: Connecting with Spirit to Transform Your Inner and Outer Worlds, 6-CD audio program
(Sounds True 2013)

Shamanic Visioning Music: Taiko Drum Journeys
(Sounds True 2014)

The Spirit of Healing: Shamanic Journey Music
(with Byron Metcalf) (Sounds True 2015)

App
Transmutation App for Apple and Android Devices

Acknowledgements

It has been a true delight to work with Katherine Wood on *The Hidden Worlds*. I wrote a story based on my own spiritual guidance to share a shamanic foundation with children and young adults. Our children are our future and need and deserve a way to work with the personal and planetary challenges they are facing in life. Katherine took the *skeleton* foundation of the story I wrote and helped me to create an engaging teaching adventure for all who read this inspirited book.

I also want to give deep gratitude to Barb Haas who helped as we were bringing more life to the characters and to the plot of the original story I had written.

I want to thank everyone at Moon Books and John Hunt Publishing for their support of our work and their brilliant help with birthing this book into the world.

I am always so grateful for my agent Barbara Moulton who tirelessly supports all my books and projects and helps and supports me on so many levels.

And I hold such deep love and give thanks to my husband, Woods Shoemaker, for his patience and support when I get so involved in my writing projects.

I also give thanks to the characters that showed up in my dreams and visions, who wanted their voices and stories to be shared.

Sandra Ingerman

Sandra Ingerman has been my teacher for almost a decade, and I have so much for which to be grateful to her. I thank her for trusting me with her idea and allowing me to work with Isaiah and Company to bring forth their story which I know will touch the lives of our readers.

I thank my grandson, Carter Lusk, who, with red pen in hand, made suggestions. He did not want to leave in the part about the big ass truck, but Rose won out.

I, too, thank Barbara Haas for her early input and Denise Vega for her wonderful questions that led to the final draft. I also thank Imelda Almquist for guiding us to John Hunt Publishing and Moon Books, and I thank all of the people who helped us there for their patience and wonderful suggestions.

Finally, I thank Julie Lusk and Cheryl Linden for their undying faith in my writing, and I thank all of my former students—31 years' worth—for their reading and writing suggestions. Here's your reading homework!

Katherine Wood

Chapter 1

Chain Reactions

Math problems finished, Isaiah dropped his forehead onto his desk. His face flushed against the cool desktop as he recalled the breakfast exchange with his mom. The instant replay ran in full Technicolor across Isaiah's closed eyelids:

"Klick. Klack." His mother's teeth snapped together—the warning sound to be on alert for something embarrassing.

"I just read an article about the concerns boys have with puberty."

Puberty? At breakfast? Missing his dad volted through him. Why wasn't he here right now? Without looking up, Isaiah poked out the center of the sunny-side-up egg with his toast. Yoke spread yellow across the plate.

"Your testicles will double in size and may be uneven meaning one may hang down farther than the other."

Isaiah noticed how powder rose, hovering just above her oatmeal as she plopped a spoonful of protein into it. He wished he could rise up and leave the kitchen. His face was hot. She stirred, apparently waiting for a response.

"Okay," he croaked, feeling certain that if one of his testicles was lower than the other, he'd never ever tell her.

"Your voice cracking is normal too," she said. "Your voice box is enlarging, and your vocal cords are stretching. It's embarrassing and annoying but will eventually go away."

Isaiah thought his voice changing was more than annoying. He was used to not being able to trust his asthmatic body, but now he couldn't rely on his voice either. He never knew when it would be high or low or both in the same word. And puberty and everything enlarging?

His mom was still speaking. "...involuntary erections..."

"I have to brush my teeth," he said, standing so quickly he knocked his chair over.

"Wait!" his mother said using her no-nonsense voice. "It is time for you to start wearing deodorant." She placed a container on the table. Isaiah noticed it was the same brand she used. Was that right? From commercials on TV, he didn't think men and women wore the same deodorant. "It has no animal ingredients and there's been no animal testing with this product," she added.

If he had to wear deodorant, at least it was one that hadn't harmed any animals. The container said 'Natural Fragrance' but right below that was the word 'calendula'. Didn't that have something to do with marigolds? Great.

With his head still against the desk, Isaiah fanned his shirt under his armpits and sniffed at the air. He didn't smell flowers.

The classroom door squeaked open, and Isaiah watched the boy named George enter. As George's special services teacher waved goodbye to him, Isaiah heard several boys in the back of the room laugh. George dropped his head, pushed his sliding glasses back against his nose, and returned to his seat. Isaiah felt sorry for George.

"Shut your faces!" Rose, a girl two rows over, said twisting around, her magenta and black hair flying. Isaiah admired her courage in speaking up, but she often got sent to the hall for it, or the principal's office.

"That will be enough all of you," his math teacher said.

Isaiah was glad he was invisible to his meaner classmates so he didn't have to put up with what George did. He just wished the others saw him as more than the weak kid with breathing issues.

"I'd like to correct our problems, please," Magda said to their teacher. Magda was planning on getting a soccer scholarship so she often redirected the class. Isaiah admired how easily Magda could boss people around, especially adults. She probably got to pick out her own deodorant.

The teacher smiled at her. "Okay everyone; it's time to check your work."

The next period, their science teacher explained that they were going to be learning the difference between physical and chemical reactions. With their lab partners they were going to do an experiment to make their own cold packs to demonstrate a physical reaction.

Isaiah wrote in his notebook, "A physical reaction is one where the matter stays the same, but the size, shape or appearance of the matter changes."

His lab partner said, "I'll get the ammonium nitrate, plastic storage bag, and graduated cylinder." He was already halfway across the room and called back, "You get the aprons, gloves, and goggles."

Isaiah wanted to say, "I wear deodorant now so I should get the ammonium nitrate." But he wasn't brave enough. It did help a little to notice the goggles were marked 'chemical resistant'. That made his job seem a little more daring.

"I'll measure out the 25 grams of ammonium nitrate into the bag," he heard himself saying a few minutes later.

His lab partner stared at him and then grabbed the graduated cylinder to measure out 50 milliliters of water which he quickly poured into the bag. He took the bag from Isaiah, released the excess air, pressed the bag tabs closed, and began squeezing it to mix the water with the ammonium nitrate.

Isaiah thought his lab partner was working quickly just in case Isaiah tried to do anything else. He was proud of himself for speaking up for once. And his voice hadn't cracked.

"Whoa! It's getting cold," his lab partner said. He handed the bag to Isaiah. It really did feel like an ice pack. Soon kids were parading around the room with their bags on their foreheads, backs, shoulders, and arms.

"Take your seats," the science teacher yelled. "As you can see from this experiment, everything is inter-related or connected, and by combining different types of matter, a physical reaction can occur. The ammonium nitrate stayed the same. The water stayed the same but putting them together changed the temperature. Our choices to put different matter together can create changes that impact everything around us."

Isaiah thought about how in math class George walking in the door had created a chain reaction. Just like his parents' divorce meant his dad moved to Denver which led to his mother being the one to have the talk with him this morning. A chain of events that could possibly lead to flowering armpits.

"It's very helpful for a soccer player to know how to make an ice pack in case there aren't any around," Magda was saying.

"You might have difficulty finding a good supply of ammonium nitrate," blurted George. Isaiah noticed the silence that followed George's comment. Isaiah couldn't remember ever hearing his voice before. Then Isaiah heard someone mutter something unintelligible. Probably the same kid from math.

And Rose was on her feet. Magda also stood and stepped in front of her. "Let's do the next experiment," she said, never taking her eyes off of Rose.

"This isn't over," went through Isaiah's mind as he watched Rose sit down, glaring back at Magda the whole time. "Deodorant and drama," he thought. "Glad it's Friday."

Saturday mornings were Isaiah's favorite time of the week. He would jump out of bed, grab his favorite cereal and milk, and head for the family room for hours of video games. It was the only time he was allowed to do three things: stay in his pajamas until noon, eat his favorite sugary, magically delicious cereal (a whole box if he wanted it), and play video games. The only thing that could make Saturday mornings more perfect was to share them with a dog, but because of his asthma, he wasn't allowed to have one. That didn't stop him from reading book after book about training dogs and picking out names. Currently his dog would be Lucky.

This Saturday, right before he left his bedroom, he thought again about breakfast yesterday and somehow it didn't feel right to go to the family room in his PJs. He pulled on a pair of sweatpants over his pyjama bottoms.

At noon each Saturday when she wasn't working, his mother vacuumed. Everywhere. At noon he was expected to put away his games, eat the sandwich she always had waiting for him on the kitchen counter, do his chores (put his laundry by the washer, clean his bathroom, and take out the recycling), and start on his homework. Saturday night they always ordered pizza and watched a movie, and Sundays were family time (church and playing board games) so his mother wanted all homework and chores done by the six o'clock pizza delivery on Saturday.

Isaiah opened his notebook at the counter while he ate his sandwich. He hoped this would discourage his mother from discussing puberty further. He looked really busy each time she came through the kitchen.

For science, he had to write up the lab report for the second experiment they had done on a chemical reaction—again in a plastic bag—using calcium chloride. He wanted to note that he was the one who had collected the calcium chloride. That meant his lab partner only got to pick up the sodium bicarbonate (a fancy name for baking soda) and the cabbage juice. It had been cool to watch the color turn from blue-green to purple to pink when they were all mixed and how the bag inflated with gas and got hot and then cold. A chemical reaction because the color changed, and it became a gas.

He also needed to collect a water sample from home or around town to be tested during lab time next week. He found a little jar and loaded it with tap water from his kitchen sink. Boring old tap water, he thought. He wished he knew somewhere to get water that might be exciting to test.

For math, he had to create a graph on world population growth since records had been kept. On graph paper, he put the years across the bottom and the population numbers along the sides. He was surprised how quickly the population had grown from 1900 to 7.4 billion today. He then had to explain one possible effect that the growing population has had on the world. He wrote that more laws were needed to control bigger groups of people. He guessed even with more laws it was easier to get away with crimes in cities; different from his small town. One of the reasons Isaiah's mom said she liked their small town was that crime couldn't exist because everyone knew everyone else's business.

His language arts teacher had said she would be assigning groups of four on Monday for a cause-effect project. He wondered what that might be.

As he did his chores, his dread grew about working with a group of four in language arts. He didn't have any friends. At least his teacher was assigning groups so he wouldn't have to be embarrassed when he didn't get picked. He had struggled with team work all through elementary school. It had really made him feel invisible. Maybe in middle school it would be different.

Chapter 2

The Dream

In his dream, thick yellow air surrounded Isaiah, hanging like blankets as if to block his way. Burning his eyes. Filling his mouth with a foul taste. He ran trying to escape it, his asthma causing him to suck in big gulps. His throat felt furry. His lungs were heavy, as if filled with hot cotton. He coughed trying to expel the dirty air.

In a pond beside him, dead fish floated belly up, bloated and white. Their lifeless eyes drifted on the bittersweet water. There were so many of them.

Looking down, Isaiah saw his feet picking their way around dead birds, black and swollen, covering the ground, their red wings still. Something had killed the birds too.

Scared of not being able to breathe at all in this nightmare, scared of the floating eyes of the fish, scared of the bloated bird bodies, Isaiah ran faster, trying to escape.

Sudden trembling happened in the dreamscape, almost as if he had broken through a barrier, and Isaiah found himself in a forest sitting, cross legged, in a circle around a campfire with three other kids. The putrid air had cleared. His lungs no longer hurt, and he could breathe normally again. Tall cottonwoods, aspen trees and pines encircled them. The fire was shooting sparks of light around them. And the dead fish and birds had disappeared.

The others were shimmering. It was like they were there and weren't at the same time. He looked down at his own hands. One minute he could see right through them and the next minute, he couldn't. The others seemed familiar, like kids at school, but he couldn't quite name them.

There were animals too. A grizzly standing on his hind legs. An octopus. A giraffe. A black panther circling the perimeter. They were solid. Isaiah felt protection coming from them.

And it was very quiet. He couldn't even hear the fire snapping or crackling, although it was burning brightly. Every so often a log would splinter into light and collapse into the center, but there was no familiar popping sound. He couldn't even hear his own breathing.

A loud cough interrupted his thoughts. He looked up, startled by this sudden sound. The cottonwoods had moved closer to him. They had eyes, noses, and mouths. They were staring at him. Their long branches reached around him.

"Pay attention!" one old cottonwood tree grumbled, shaking him with a branch. "Pay attention! Pay attention!" The other trees picked up the chant. "Pay attention!"

Chapter 3

The Discovery

"Isaiah, pay attention!" his teacher said. Isaiah sat up at his desk. Suddenly, he remembered his dream from last night and the trees telling him to pay attention. A kind of queasy feeling hit his stomach thinking about the dead birds and fish. "Isaiah, the bell rang, and everyone has gone to lunch. I know it's Monday, but get with it!" Now how did he miss the bell for lunch? That was his favorite time of the day.

Outside, a group of boys jostled him as they passed on their way up to the football field. "Yep, I'm still invisible," he thought. "So far middle school has been no different."

Isaiah located the lunch monitor. Her back was turned, so he used the chance to slip through the cottonwood trees at the edge of the school grounds. He headed for the pond.

He found his favorite log and dropped to the ground, resting against it. He wiggled around so nothing was poking into his skinny back. He lifted his pale face to the sun and sighed, running his hands through his white-blond hair. *"Pay attention!"* What had happened after the trees had chanted that?

The sound of someone crying nearby made Isaiah snap open his eyes.

George was slumped on the other end of the log, his big belly heaving with sobs.

"Are you okay?" Isaiah asked softly.

George wiped under his nose, trailing snot along his hand. He nodded shyly, his glasses fogged over. "My-my-my mom says someday I'll be a swan and not to worry about my ugly duckling phase, but I don't think she knows how mean kids can be." He ended in a whisper. George dropped his head into his hands.

Isaiah felt sorry for George, but at least George wasn't invisible.

Before Isaiah could respond, an angry shout came from inside the cottonwoods. Two girls locked in a fight of hair pulling and punching fell onto the ground near them.

"Take it back right now!" Rose yelled.

Magda had her hands clenched in Rose's black and neon green streaked hair. She was trying to pull her off. "Rose, you are from China. Why does that make you so mad?"

"Shut up, Magda!" Rose had her hands wrapped around Magda's black ponytail, tugging. Her matching neon green fingernails wove in and out of Magda's curls. "You're such a butt kisser. 'Let's correct our math problems now'," Rose mimicked.

So this wasn't about China. It was payback for their confrontation on Friday.

"Get off of me!" Magda said. She lifted upward and twisted, throwing Rose. Magda played league soccer, so she was strong. Rose flew forward.

She landed on her hands and knees, screaming as she lifted her right hand into the air, shaking something black and gooey off of it. She jerked and ran toward the other kids, still screaming. "What is it? Get it off of me!"

"Here. Let me see." Isaiah took Rose's hand into his. It was covered in blood and black feathers. He pulled a tissue from his back pocket and wiped her hand clean.

Magda called from the spot where Rose had fallen, "Disgusting! It's a dead bird! You fell on a dead bird!"

Rose started screaming again, the fight with Magda already in the past.

George lumbered over to Magda, his tears drying. He squatted down and poked the bird with a stick. "Dead all right," he said. He stood and scanned the area. "Whoa! There's another dead one over there."

"And over there," Magda pointed.

The four of them spread out, searching the area, calling out as they found the birds. Isaiah felt his throat constricting with tears. All of these beautiful birds, lying lifeless on the ground. No longer riding the air currents, calling out from tree to tree, the red and yellow wings gone still in death.

When an eagle cried, they all looked up. It was swooping around a lone blackbird which was making a struggling flight. It dropped closer and closer to the ground. It tried to land, but its wings seemed suddenly too heavy to flap. It hit the ground with a quiet thunk.

They circled the blackbird as the eagle continued to call from above. Its side lifted rapidly up and down. One black eye looked up at them imploringly.

"We have to help it," Magda cried.

Rose bent down. "We'll take it to the vet."

George squatted beside her. "Hey little one, you'll be okay. We're here to help. Don't be scared." He brushed together a pile of leaves. Gently, he slid his fingers beneath the bird and lifted it onto the little bed. He ran an index finger over the top of its head and down along its back, smoothing the shiny black feathers. The bird blinked.

Rose stroked the bird next. "So sweet," she whispered.

Isaiah brushed tears from his eyes.

And then a puff of air released from the bird and its chest quit moving. The eye stopped blinking.

A single eagle feather left its giant wing, gliding down, down until it came tenderly to rest atop the fallen blackbird.

Like a prayer, Isaiah thought. *The bird died literally at our feet.* And then he remembered. "We have to go and look at the pond!" he yelled. He knew that dead fish would be floating belly up on the water, like in his dream.

"What happened to them?" Rose asked as they stood on the banks looking at the gelatinous, unmoving bodies of the fish. The smell of rot was overpowering.

"It looks like some type of environmental poisoning," George announced, his brown eyes serious. "Probably what happened to all these birds too. I have read about these things before."

They all stared at George.

He stammered, "I'm going to be a scientist when I grow up." He ducked his head down. "My dad dreams of me being a professional athlete, but you can see how that's turning out." George smiled at his own joke. "Hey—we need to tell the lunch monitor."

"No frickin' way," shouted Rose. "We're off the school grounds, and Magda and I were fighting. We'll get in a ton of trouble."

"But someone has to do something about this," George said.

He just stood up to Rose, Isaiah thought.

The lunch bell rang in the distance.

Magda said, "I agree with Rose. No one tells anyone anything until we've talked about this more." She turned toward the school.

Now she agrees with Rose? Isaiah needed to think about how this chain reaction which began with a fist fight had led to the two girls agreeing.

"We do need to get back," Isaiah said. "Let's meet here at lunch tomorrow so we can talk more. Then we will ask for help." He patted George on the back, and as he hurried back to class, Isaiah noticed that his asthma hadn't flared up when he was running around looking at the dead birds and fish.

Chapter 4

Recognition

A gentle feathered-wing brushed across Isaiah's eyes. In his dream, he opened them slowly. On a branch in a cottonwood tree, an eagle perched. He was staring at Isaiah. Isaiah felt as if this eagle had a message for him.

The eagle looked far into a field. Isaiah followed his gaze. There was a parade coming! In the lead was a bear. Its size reminded him of Pathfinder, the six-foot tall, bronze grizzly sculpture on the college campus—but this bear was walking on his hind legs and throwing candy.

Behind the bear were two drum majorettes carrying a sign that read 'Power Animal Parade'. A giraffe was next. He was wearing a t-shirt that said 'Protect, Heal, Advise'. A black panther with green eyes came from the back and circled the parade, looking side to side and behind. At the end was an octopus which was scooping up the candy and launching it again. The animals from his last dream. He recognized them.

"Power animals?" Isaiah asked himself looking again at their sign as the parade drew closer.

"I've heard about animal friends," a girl beside him said. "They live in the hidden realms. Supposedly everyone has at least one animal guardian spirit."

Isaiah turned around, startled. He had thought he was in his dream alone. It was Rose who had spoken! Magda and George were here too! How was this happening?

Rose added, "I wonder if these are our guardian spirits? Let's close our eyes and ask them to come to us."

Isaiah didn't know what was going on, but he played along with the dream. "If we all do that at the same time, there'll be a bunch of animals, so how will we know which one belongs to each of us?"

"I think we'll just know," Magda said closing her eyes.

When Isaiah opened his eyes, the great grizzly bear who had been leading the parade stood beside him. The parade had disbanded and the drum majorettes were gone. So was the candy.

The octopus sat beside George, several of her tentacles wrapped around his shoulders.

The giraffe in the t-shirt sat next to Rose.

And Magda had a look of despair on her face. "I don't have an animal."

"Yes, you do," Isaiah told her. "It's a beautiful black panther with bright green eyes."

"Why can't I see him?" Magda asked.

George said, "Can you feel a panther near you?"

Magda closed her eyes and her smile turned as radiant as the shining sun. "I feel him circling me," she whispered. "He's so graceful, so beautiful!

"Are you my power animal?" The big cat nudged her with his head.

"Are each of these power animals?" Isaiah asked the big bear who nodded his head.

Rose turned to her giraffe and said, "How's a giraffe going to protect, heal and advise me? I get in a lot of trouble."

No answer came from Giraffe. Isaiah could see Rose's face turning angry.

"Rose," Magda said, "try feeling the answer or hearing it inside of you."

Rose swallowed and closed her eyes.

She jumped up a few minutes later. "Guys, it worked! I listened in a way I've never tried before, and I heard Giraffe say, 'We will communicate from the inside. Yes, Rose, I'll help you. You just need to ask.' I couldn't hear her before, but now I can."

George turned to the others holding his arms up in the air. "Why did I get an octopus?"

Octopus wrapped all of her tentacles around George and said, "I will help you become a great scientist." Then she lifted George right off *of the ground. He and Octopus were flying!*

George yelled back, "My octopus can fly!" Then, "Things really look different from here, guys. It's cool!"

"Wait for me," cried Isaiah, as Grizzly Bear gently carried him up into the air as well.

Rose jumped onto Giraffe's back and Magda and Panther followed.

Isaiah felt the strength and power of this bear, his bear. What else can these amazing animals do he wondered.

When they softly landed, he felt the love in Grizzly's paws as he hugged Isaiah. "I'm excited to learn more about why you're here."

"You're coming of age," Grizzly said. "You'll need our help." With that, the parade reassembled and moved again into the distance. Eagle, who had observed it all, nodded once and with a strong swoop of his wings, flew into the air.

Chapter 5

Eavesdropping

Isaiah's language arts teacher was reading off groups. She had matched them alphabetically.

"Isaiah Dunfrey, Magda Duncan, George Dunrite, Maribel Engel." So Isaiah was in a group with George and Magda. Maribel was a blonde beauty who giggled all of the time. Rose Wilson was in another group. A group with three of the guys who made comments from the back of the room.

"There will be no changes so don't ask. Groups will begin meeting tomorrow. With your group, you'll choose a cause-effect topic off of a list. You'll research it and create a cause-effect PowerPoint which you'll present to the class."

At lunch, Isaiah slipped between the cottonwoods and ran to the pond. All morning in their core classes the kids had exchanged glances with each other, especially in language arts when the groups were announced. *I wonder if we all know we shared the dream?* Isaiah kept thinking.

Magda and Rose were already there. Rose was poking dead fish with a stick, and Magda looked a little sick.

"Where's George?" Isaiah asked the girls.

"I saw him leave when we did," Magda said.

Rose dropped the stick and squinted toward the school. "Here he comes! By the way, I am making a plan to get kicked out of my group so that Maribel and I can trade."

George ambled up, out of breath. "Where are the animals?" he asked.

"The animals?" Isaiah said. *The animals from the dream?*

"Yeah, last night I had this dream. I had an octopus…" "I had a giraffe who couldn't talk, but I could hear her in my head!" Rose shouted. "Magda, you had a black…"

"Panther. And I had a bear," Isaiah said. "Magda, did you have the same dream as us?"

Magda shook her head. "I don't believe in dreams. Besides animals can't fly."

"So you did have it!" Rose said. "My giraffe flew just fine, thank you very much."

"It was just a dream," Magda said.

"But we all had it. The same dream. Don't you think that's weird?" Rose said.

"I guess." Magda shrugged.

"But my octopus said she's going to help me be a good student, and I believe her," George said.

"We all had the same dream so that must mean something really important. The animals are here to help us," Isaiah said. When he spoke, the others stopped and listened.

"We have to get more than our dream animals involved in this," George said. "We have to tell some adults about the birds and fish."

Just then the eagle flew over them and cried. "Let's follow him," Isaiah said. The eagle dipped over the small stream that fed the pond. "He wants us to follow the water. Maybe he's going to show us what killed the birds and fish."

"He is!" George shouted. "What killed the fish probably came from upstream." In his excitement, George's right foot slipped off of the slimy side of the stream and into the water. "I hope whatever's in this water won't hurt my foot," he said as he lifted his tennis shoe out of the mucky water. "It stinks here worse than a swamp."

They followed Eagle for a few minutes. Soon the cottonwood access from the school yard was in the distance. Up ahead, the stream ran under a big fence.

"It looks like the fence is around a building of some sort," Isaiah said, leading the group. He was surprised that he wasn't out of breath. His asthma still seemed to be under control.

At the back of the fence, they found a gate leading into the grounds. It seemed to be locked on the inside.

"How are we going to get inside so we can keep following the stream?" George asked.

Without a thought, Magda quickly climbed the fence, she swung the gate open for the others.

"Let's prop it open with this rock so we can get out quickly if we need to," Isaiah said, putting a large stone in the opening. "Thanks, Magda!"

"No problem," she said. "I felt like I flew up and over that fence. It was strange."

Isaiah nodded, remembering what it was like to fly in his dream. He looked around. There was a low shed up ahead, surrounded by dirty barrels and rusted metal machinery. It looked deserted. He led the group up to it so they were sheltered from a large metal warehouse ahead.

"I think we can make our way across the yard to get back to the stream by staying behind stuff just in case there's someone in that big building," Isaiah instructed. They began picking their way toward the stream.

"Look over there where the stream goes," Rose said. She pointed to more barrels which were stacked up by the stream.

Eagle circled above the barrels.

"I don't know what's going on inside this fence," said George. "But one thing's for sure. All of those barrels contain some type of poison. See the skull and crossbones on them?" He stopped. "Oh boy, we've got company."

Three men came out of the warehouse and stood behind it.

"Cigarette break," Isaiah said, "Get down!" He dropped behind some containers and held his index finger against his lips.

They could barely hear what the men were saying. "Gotta dump at least six a day... plow the lake under by next week... no trace... same pay as last time..." The kids looked at each other, and then Isaiah's throat constricted. Breathing was difficult. No matter how much air he tried to suck in, very little flowed to his lungs.

Magda heard his ragged breath and signaled to Rose and George. Isaiah slumped over, gasping.

"Where's your inhaler?" George asked going through Isaiah's pockets.

Isaiah soon felt the plastic in his mouth and as he pulled in the air, he swore he heard a very soft growl in his ear. Was Grizzly nearby? He sat up.

Keeping down low, the three of them worked together to pull him back to the gate and outside the compound. They hurried but were careful to be quiet.

"That was close! Too close!" Rose said. "Are you okay, Isaiah?"

Isaiah nodded. "Thanks, guys!"

"Did you hear what the men said?" Rose asked.

"They're dumping those barrels into the stream. That must be what is flowing down to the pond!" Magda said.

"I wonder what kind of chemicals are in them?" George asked, looking at his shoe which was still wet from his earlier slip.

"What can we do?" asked Rose.

"They're going to plow under the pond," Magda said. "What about the cottonwoods and all the animals that depend on that water?"

"Right now we need to get back to school. Lunch should be almost over," Isaiah said. George slipped under Isaiah's arm to help support him. Magda got under his other arm.

Rose kicked rocks. "That's a bunch of crap!" A rock flew up. "It makes me so mad," she said, launching another rock right after it. "Dumping poison. Killing fish. Killing birds. Taking away the pond." She stopped kicking and said, "We have to stop them!"

"I agree," Magda said. "There has to be something we can do.

Maybe we can tell the mayor or the police."

"May I point out again that we'll get in trouble (effect) for being off the school grounds during lunch (cause)?" Rose asked. "I know, since breaking school rules is kind of my specialty. I don't want to get busted when, this time, I was doing something good. We can't tell our parents for the same reason."

"We could call the owner and tell him what those men are doing," Isaiah said.

George said, "It's very expensive to get rid of waste like that. The owner might be in on it to save money. We really don't know who's involved. This could be a very dangerous situation. Maybe we should report it to the Environmental Protection Agency."

"They won't believe us because we're children," Rose said making air quotes around 'children' and kicking another rock.

"Maybe we need to get some more information. Maybe wait and see what happens tonight in our dreams," said Isaiah, remembering what Grizzly had told him about an important job. "Eagle led us here. Maybe our animals have information we need."

"Maybe we can somehow tie all of this into our language arts project," Magda added.

"You can't make it too obvious!" Rose shouted. "Besides she said we'd be choosing off of a list. I doubt this is on the list."

Isaiah turned to Rose, "You have to be in our group."

"Don't worry. Getting kicked out of places is another specialty," Rose said.

Over tuna casserole that night, Isaiah said, "Mom, do you know anything about that big warehouse near my school?"

His mother had lived in this small mountain town of five thousand souls all of her life. He loved her stories about the town's history and how she always joked that Main Street was wide enough to turn your mule and wagon around. She knew lots of history, and he'd grown up hearing stories about the outlaw Wyatt Earp. He'd escaped the law in Arizona and set up camp on the outskirts of town. After the Colorado governor refused to turn him over, Wyatt had settled in town, running Faro, a gambling card game. Once when Isaiah had been in the hospital, his mother had taught him to play Faro. They'd used his Pokemon cards for chips, and he went broke real quick.

But for all of her love of town lore, his mother was also suspicious. That's probably what made her such a good research librarian at the college. "Why do you want to know about that building?" She lowered her fork and stared at Isaiah.

"I'm just curious what they do there." He'd already practiced what to say so she wouldn't get alarmed. It made him feel like Wyatt Earp. "I wonder every time the bus goes by it. I just remembered to ask tonight, that's all." He gave her what he thought the neutral outlaw look would be when caught with the bank's gold in his hands.

She seemed to buy his explanation. "It was originally built as a tanning plant for hunters who wanted to keep their deer and elk hides. Then it was a small machines' repair business. Some college students did a spot on the radio recently about the property having been purchased by a new business that gets rid of hazardous waste. That place has been an eyesore for years. I hope they clean it up.

"Hazardous waste?" Isaiah asked. His heart raced.

"Yes, I've heard that businesses pay a lot of money to get rid of toxic substances. I am glad there is a business here in town that can do that properly without hurting the environment."

Isaiah had stopped listening. Those men had been talking about dumping six barrels of toxic chemicals a day into the stream! Even more fish would die. He realized his mother was studying him. Back to Wyatt Earp pretend innocence.

"How was your asthma today?" she asked.

"I had a little flare up at lunch," he said, feeling a bit guilty for not telling her the whole truth.

"Were you running?" she asked.

"No, I was being careful."

"Maybe it's getting too cold outside, and you should stay in."

"Mom, it's only the beginning of October! It's not like it's winter time yet." Their town was at an elevation of 7,700 feet and was in a valley so it was known for the cold that settled into it. Sometimes it was the coldest place in the nation.

"I just worry," she sighed as she brushed her hand across his bangs.

Chapter 6

Meeting Jeremiah

"Hey!" *Isaiah heard a tiny voice call out from a small opening in the rocks. A little salamander stood at the opening of a cave. He had on a backwards baseball cap.*

"Jeremiah! Come back in here!" The salamander's mother came running out yelling. Her over-protectiveness reminded Isaiah of his own mother.

"It's okay, Mama. Eagle brought them." Jeremiah jumped up on a rock. "Would you all like to come in and see my house?" He pointed to the tiny cave below him.

Isaiah became aware that the others were in his dream again.

"How can we get into such a tiny house? We're too big," said Magda.

Isaiah said, "I remember from my first dream that my body wasn't solid. Maybe we can shrink our bodies to fit."

"Now that's an idea I'd like to try," George laughed, smacking his thick thigh.

Isaiah thought himself smaller and smaller. Soon he was standing beside Jeremiah, and they were the same size.

The others watched in complete amazement. They were inspired to try it.

"Wow! Look how little I am!" George shouted. He began dancing with Octopus who also had shrunk.

Soon everyone followed Jeremiah into his home. It was a simple home, filled with rocks and grasses. Isaiah felt a sense of peace here.

Jeremiah scooted across the cool, dirt floor. "I'd take you to my bedroom, but, well, it's a mess." His mother cleared her throat, and he shrugged at her. "Maybe next time you come I can show you my Super Sally Salamander comic book collection. Let's sit here."

As they settled onto rock furniture, Jeremiah said, "We're not so different you know. I mean, we definitely look different, but we all live on this great earth together." He looked around at each of them. *"Oh! I'm just so happy Eagle has brought you here. You're my first human friends."*

Jeremiah's mother passed around a tiny tray of nut-berry bars. As the others thanked her, Isaiah asked, *"Has Eagle brought us to you so you can help with our problem?"*

"Yes, you've discovered something that's hurting fish, birds, trees, the Earth, air, water—all of us. There's something you can do while you figure out the big solution," Jeremiah said. *"Super Sally says we have to protect the water because it supports life for everything. Actually, she's the inspiration for my idea. She travels where most salamanders dare not go."*

"What's your idea?" Isaiah asked.

"Follow me, and I'll show you." He turned to George. *"You and Octopus will be super important in making this idea work because you already thought of this."*

In very little time, they were gathered inside the fence at the factory next to the stream. They were still salamander-sized.

"George, you, me and Octopus are going to dive into the water so we can swim beside the hose that's dumping the poison. We need to pull the hose off of the barrel, and switch the valve into a closed position. That will shut off the flow. We'll replace the hose, and hopefully, no one will notice for a while that the barrel is plugged."

"I did think about that today! How did you know?" George asked.

"We are connected, my man," Jeremiah said, tapping fists with him.

"Cool," George said. *"Which part do you need to me do?"*

"Octopus is going to pull off the hose and hold it. All of her arms will be good in keeping it steady so it doesn't float off downstream. You will close the valve. I want you to see up close what's involved so that you can do it outside of dream time," Jeremiah answered.

"Outside of dream time? You mean at lunch?" George's voice shook. *"Will I have to go into the water that's poisoned?"*

"Not tomorrow," Jeremiah said. *"Tonight you'll see how it works*

up close and personal—and underwater. Don't worry—you'll be protected from the poison. Tomorrow you'll have to do it all by feel since you'll be on the bank and working upside down. And you'll be wearing a long pair of rubber gloves that you'll need to bring. You don't want any of the water to get on you."

"Oh boy," George said.

"I'll bring rubber gloves," Rose said. "The cleaning service my mother uses keeps lots of new packages of them in our cupboard."

"And I'll help you with my extra hands," said Octopus, wrapping several of them around George, reassuring him.

Jeremiah laughed. "George, yes, we need your hands to do the work tomorrow. That's why you need to go into the water to see what's what. Pay close attention and get the feel of the valve and how to close it. Now, while we swim, Octopus, you need to hold these masks in front of our faces. That will keep the poison away. And George, leave your glasses on so you can see."

"What do you need us to do up here?" asked Isaiah.

"You're the lookouts. Usually no one's around at night, but just in case. Stay between the barrels. Pull on the hose if someone comes."

"Giraffe says we're ready," salamander-sized Rose announced from atop Giraffe, her voice tiny.

"Please be careful everyone even though we are hard to see," Magda said. Then she added, "I just felt Panther growl. I think he agrees with me."

"Here's to Super Sally," Jeremiah said as he dove into the water. George looked like he wanted to turn and run, but Octopus pulled him down into the polluted stream.

In what felt like seconds, they were back. "Thumbs up! Operation Learn to Close the Barrel accomplished. Let's get out of here," George whispered.

They landed outside of Jeremiah's cave. "Thanks for showing me how to make my idea work," George said, bumping fists with Jeremiah again.

"You have great ideas," Rose said to George.

Isaiah noticed that George's cheeks got a little red, but he didn't duck his head down. Instead he smiled at Rose. "Thanks."

"The trick will work to buy you some time while you figure out what to do. May Super Sally go with you!" Jeremiah called after them.

Chapter 7

Following Instructions

"I like choice number seven," Magda said as they looked over the choices for their cause-effect project in language arts on Wednesday. "Popularity of Sports in the US. We could always narrow it down to soccer."

"I would rather do number twelve on the Impact of Fashion Choices. What you wear has a lot to do with how you're treated," Maribel said, looking at Magda's sweatpants.

Isaiah was stuck at three: The Causes and Effects of Divorces. And number four: Growing Up with a Single Parent. There had to be some better topics.

"Let's skip the Effects of School Bullying since it might get one of us hurt," George said.

Suddenly, a loud argument erupted from the back of the room. Isaiah saw Rose on her feet. "You three aren't even trying to be serious. My grade matters to me, so we need to discuss which of these topics will work for us."

One of the boys said, "That's just because no one would want to date you," and the boys in the group started laughing loudly.

Rose looked at the teacher. "Dating at a young age is not the best topic for immature seventh grade boys."

"Maribel, they're friends of yours. Do you think you could work with them?" Isaiah heard himself saying.

Maribel raised her hand and said, "I can keep them on task. Why don't Rose and I trade? You guys'll do number twelve, right?"

The teacher nodded, apparently choosing peace over her no trading rule.

Rose slid into their group, her neon yellow hair bouncing. "Told you I could get out of that asinine group. Now since I know nothing about How Happy Relationships Affect a Person, maybe we should do that one." She pointed to eighteen. Then she crisscrossed number nineteen: The Cause and Effect of Telling Lies. "Better not do that one."

George pulled out a piece of notebook paper. "What about number thirteen? The Cause and Effect of the Environment on Animals/Animals on the Environment? I'm sure we'd have some help from you know who."

Magda looked up from the list. "That's a great idea. We could each focus on our particular power animal and research all about them. That would be fun."

"Great idea, George," Isaiah said.

As George wrote it down, Rose said, "I'm okay if we stick to our animals. We just can't go dragging our local birds and fish into it. At least not yet."

At lunch, after they relived last night's adventure with Jeremiah, Isaiah told the others what he'd learned from his mother. "During dream time, I wondered if I could have told you about the hazardous waste and if you would have remembered. I decided to wait until we were awake," he concluded.

"We should experiment with that," George suggested. "Anyway, now we have proof that what's going on is really, really bad. We need to tell someone."

"Magda said, "Hey—I heard my parents talking about the new company, but I didn't pay that much attention. My dad's college roommate, my Uncle Robb, is the one who bought it. He lives in Kansas City."

"I wish my parents talked about things like that at dinner," George said, side-tracked for a minute. "All I hear about is college sports. Basketball this. Football that. Up and coming track stars. Division Two play offs. Fifteen national championships. Eighty-nine Rocky Mountain Athletic Conference Championships since 1911. Blah. Blah. Blah."

"At least your parents are home to have dinner with you,"

spiked Rose. "Ever since I ran off the last nanny, I'm home alone breakfast, lunch and dinner."

Isaiah wanted to say something about having two parents at dinner but didn't. His father had moved to Denver after the divorce. Now he rarely saw him. Changing the subject, he said, "Could you believe how we were able to get so tiny last night?"

"I wish I could do that in awake time," George sighed. "I'd never get called fat again."

Isaiah changed the subject again, "We'd better get going on Operation Close the Valve so we don't run out of time."

Rose pulled a paper from her pocket. She unfolded it. "I made this drawing from what you described last night in the dream, George. It's upside down to help you."

They looked at the detailed drawing done in black ink.

"This is beautiful, Rose," Magda said.

Rose shifted from foot to foot as if unused to compliments. "My parents are architects," she said as if that explained it. "Maybe you can follow this, George, and it'll help. Oh — and here are the gloves."

"Wow, this drawing will help a lot," George said. "No one's ever done something like this for me before." He tucked the drawing and the gloves into his backpack.

The four of them moved quietly to the fence by the gate. Isaiah reviewed the plan they'd practiced in dream time.

"George and Jeremiah came up with a good plan," Magda kicked at the yellow leaves covering the ground.

"Thanks again for the drawing, Rose," George said.

They went through the gate and looked to be sure there was no one around. Then, for the second day in a row, they ran between discarded machinery and large barrels across the compound toward the stream. There were no men outside smoking this time.

Eagle swooped down to join them when they got to the barrels.

George was shaking as he bent beside the barrel draining poison into the water. He pulled on the rubber gloves. "Ro-ro-rose," he said quietly, "can you hold the picture for me about here." He signaled eye level from his knees. Rose knelt beside him with the drawing.

"Magda and I'll be lookouts here," Isaiah whispered, squatting between the two barrels, Magda beside him. "We'll pull on the hose if we see anything." He patted George on the arm. "You can do it," he said.

George put his hand into the stream, and the others saw a shiver run up his arm. "Cold! Even with gloves," he whispered.

Rose pointed on the diagram to the place the hose connected to the barrel.

Isaiah felt time stop as he watched the building, and he watched George. This was taking forever!

Sweat was dripping into George's eyes behind his glasses. He was still shaking.

"Octopus will help," Rose quietly reminded him.

George smiled, and a few minutes later, gave the thumbs up signal.

Rose helped him up, and quickly the group made its way back to the gate. Still no sign of the men.

"You doing okay, Isaiah?" George asked as soon as they snapped the gate shut.

Isaiah smiled. "I'm great! Thanks! Tell us everything!"

"Well, I had trouble finding things upside down, but the drawing helped." He pulled off the gloves. "Then I was having lots of trouble pulling off the hose, holding it, and turning the valve. Then Rose reminded me about Octopus. I called on her, and suddenly Pop! Turn! Whoosh! And it was done. Do you think it's possible that a dream animal helped me in awake time?"

"Yes!" Magda said. "It's like when I floated up over the fence yesterday to open the gate. Wow... it's hard to believe this is really happening," Magda said. "All four of us dream the same dreams. Then we meet Jeremiah who knows George's idea, and he shows how to do it in real life." With her best soccer footwork, Magda kicked a rock all the way back to the cottonwoods. "It's all pretty unbelievable," she called back to them.

Chapter 8

The North Wind

They were standing in front of a large cave. A huge thrust of wind flew out at them blowing their clothes backwards. The air was charged, almost electric. Eagle watched, wings tucked into his side.

"Did anyone else hear that?" Rose asked looking around.

"What?" Magda asked.

"When the wind blew out, I heard a loud, booming voice say, "Welcome! I am the North Wind."

"No, I didn't hear the voice," Isaiah said. Neither George nor Magda had either.

"That's strange you didn't hear it too. Maybe it's because I'm up so high on Giraffe," Rose said.

"Or maybe it's your gift of hearing," Magda said.

"Maybe," Rose said.

Isaiah looked at Rose. "I hear what I think might be messages in the wind all the time, but it sounds like static. I think it might be talking to me, but I'm not really sure what it's saying."

Rose stared back at Isaiah. "The wind talks to me too, but I hear words. I thought everyone did."

"Nope." Isaiah smiled. "I guess this makes you our wind interpreter."

"Huh?" Rose tilted her head into the wind.

"Wind has been bringing you help with your asthma," she told Isaiah. "It has been telling your airways to open up and take it in. It has been soothing them."

Rose listened again. "The wind wants to know if we're aware of how dependent we are on air to live."

"Well I sure do," Isaiah said.

"We can only hold our breath about two minutes," George said.

"We already know we can't live without it," Magda said.

"*The wind wants to know if we're aware that it was the first living being we said hello to after we were born into this world? That our lives started with our very first breath,*" *Rose said.*

"*I thought my parents were first, but this makes sense,*" *Magda said.*

Rose leaned forward, her orange hair blowing. "*Strong winds blow across the land so they can clean the air and the earth,*" *she said.* "*They can clean us too.*"

"*How?*" *Magda asked, stroking the fur of her panther.*

"*It says it's easy. We just stand outside and ask the air to clean us. Giraffe just said that the air is able to change the energy into love. Wow! Two voices talking inside of my head at once. My therapist would have fun with this!*"

Short puffs of air popped around them.

"*What's going on?*" *George asked.*

"*The wind is laughing and so is Giraffe,*" *Rose said.*

"*It tickles,*" *laughed George. The others joined in.*

Then Rose asked the wind, "*I get pretty angry sometimes. Are you sure you're strong enough to blow my anger away?*"

A giant gust of air hit Rose, knocking her down. They all laughed.

Isaiah said, "*Rose, ask it if it knows the warehouse by our school?*"

"*It does,*" *Rose said.* "*It also said it can understand you so you can talk directly to it.*"

"*Okay.*" *Isaiah blushed and quickly summarized what they had done so far.* "*We aren't sure what to do next.*"

Rose added, "*They must be doing something to birds too because I fell on a dead one.*" *She looked at Magda and then the ground.* "*And then we found dead birds everywhere.*"

There was a sudden stillness. They looked at each other in surprise.

Grizzly whispered to Isaiah, "*Wind has gone to check out what you said.*"

Just as Isaiah was about to share this information with the others, a gust of wind blew around them.

"*Wind says it's true. It saw the barrel we plugged up. It also* discovered that something is being burned beside the warehouse which is polluting the air. But that is not what is killing the birds," Rose reported.

"Can you help clean the air or help the birds somehow?" asked George.

Rose listened. "Yes, the wind will clear the air, but it says it won't stay clean if they keep burning. As far as the birds are concerned, the wind will blow them away from the area so they aren't harmed by whatever's going on there," Rose said, "but we need to find out what's killing them."

"Thank you so much," the others said in unison.

"And thank you, Rose, for making the messages clear for us," Magda said.

"We do need to figure out what's killing the birds," Isaiah concluded. "Tomorrow during lunch, we'll meet, and scout things out." He looked at George. "And then we'll see who we need to tell."

Chapter 9

Caught!

"Day number three of no lunch," George sang. "At this rate, I might lose some weight." They slipped through the cottonwoods. "Hey—did everyone notice that we're saying things in our dreams that we remember during the day? Like Isaiah telling us to meet today at lunch?"

"That's right," Isaiah said. "Guess it works." He pulled back a tree branch for Magda.

"Lots of kids tease you about your weight, don't they?" Rose asked.

George nodded.

"If I ever hear it, I'll kick their dumb butts," Rose said, tossing her blue hair, a match to her nail polish.

"I think they get frustrated by how long it takes me to do my work. That's why I get special services—to stay caught up in all my classes."

"Why does it take you so long?" Magda asked. She quickly added, "You don't have to say if you don't want to. It's just that I've heard kids call you names before for being slow." She looked at Rose, and then said to George, "Hey, I'm sorry I never stopped them."

"That's okay," George said looking down. "I am slow. I get these ideas, and then I have to think about them and pretty soon everyone else is turning in papers, and I have barely started. My mom wanted to homeschool me, but my dad said that would hurt my chances for getting a college scholarship. He ran track in college here, and he wants me to do it too." He paused, scratching his head. "You know, I hate to run!"

They laughed with George.

"I would like to go to college here, but it's because their

environmental studies department is top ranked. Someday, when I'm a scientist, I want to work at the biological lab."

"I don't think I've ever heard you say so many sentences in a row, George," Rose said as they walked past the pond toward the fence.

"I'm glad you have big dreams," Magda said. "Naturally my big dream is to run—on a world-class soccer field."

"I dream of moving out of our Gothic Revival house that has a u-shaped floor plan, gable dormers, and a wrought iron roof cresting," Rose said doing air quotes. She used a voice like she was mimicking one of her architect parents.

They continued looking at her.

"I guess I really want to go back to China and kick the government's butts for the way they treat girl babies."

"What do they do to girl babies?" Isaiah asked.

"They think only boys have any value so families give away their girls because they can't afford to raise them since they're not worth anything."

"That's wrong!" Magda said.

"No, wrong is that I lay in a crib until I was two years old and my U.S. parents adopted me. No one cared if I lived or I died." Rose looked close to tears. "My therapist says I have a slight attachment disorder so that's why I act like I don't want any friends even though I really do."

"Rose, I didn't know," Magda said.

"Don't worry about it." Rose's voice was hard again.

At the gate, Isaiah said, "This could be very dangerous so let's stick to the plan. We're just gathering information. Meet you all back here in 15 minutes."

Fifteen minutes later, George had reported back that the valve was still closed.

Isaiah had counted three cars in the parking lot in the front of the building, and there appeared to be an office in the front. There also had been a dog lying in the sun. "It saw me but didn't move. Obviously not a guard dog," he laughed.

Magda said that looking in the windows of the warehouse, she'd discovered nothing but boxes.

And Rose wasn't back yet.

"All she had to do was scout out the back of the building," Magda said, sounding worried.

"Look!" George said.

Rose was running toward the gate as fast as she could, and right behind her was a man. "Come back here, kid!" he yelled. He stopped to pull out his phone.

Isaiah felt fear rushing into his lungs. He watched to see if the man was calling someone or taking a video. The man kept cursing and trying to use his phone.

Rose tore right through the gate and past the others. The others quickly followed. Isaiah had already removed the rock propping it open, so Magda slammed it shut as soon as they were all through it. "OMG!" she said.

"I hate to run," a running George said under his breath, "but in this case, I choose running over getting caught by that guy. He scares me."

In the background, they heard a thunk against the gate and the man yelled, "Hey!"

Once inside the cottonwoods close to the school grounds, they stopped. The fence was out of sight. George was gasping for air, and Rose was panting. But Isaiah was breathing normally.

"I can't quit shaking! That was really scary!" Magda said. "Hey, why aren't you out of breath?" she asked Isaiah.

"I don't know," Isaiah said as surprised as she was. "At first fear filled my lungs, and then everything went calm. It's almost as if something carried me."

"Grizzly!" Magda said with conviction. But Isaiah was thinking that it was Wind that was helping him right now — with moving so fast, the calm that went through him, and his breathing.

"I knew you believed even if it's weird!" Rose said as soon as she could get the words out.

"Maybe," Magda laughed. "So what happened back there?"

"Yeah," George said, "You know I might hate to run, but I think I just beat my all-time record! What happened?"

Rose took a deep breath and let it out slowly, her hand on her heart. "That was some scary crap," she said looking at Magda who nodded. "Okay, so I was checking out the back of the warehouse like we agreed, and I found this big firepit. There was smoke coming out of it, so someone has been burning something there recently."

"That must be what Wind was talking about!" George said.

Rose nodded. "Anyway, there were bags of stuff beside the pit, really old bags, and one of them was ripped open. There were these pellet things on the ground. The bag said, *Aiv...* something. At the bottom it said: *proved to cull red-winged blackbirds.* I was going to pick up some pellets to show you but saw a big CAUTION sign on the bag, so I didn't think it was a good idea to touch them. Suddenly, I realized a man was watching me. I took off running and the rest is history. It totally scared me."

"It could have been Avitrol. It would have gone through your skin. It is really poisonous! It's on the EPA's list," George informed them. He pulled off his glasses to wipe them. "I am so glad you didn't touch it, Rose. Farmers use it to kill birds because they eat their grain in the fields and in their livestock feeders."

"Well this would have been old farmers because those bags looked ancient," Rose said. "Let's not forget the man who saw me though."

Isaiah said, "We have no idea what that'll mean. That man pulled out his phone and may have gotten some video of our backs."

Rose grabbed Isaiah's arm. "Was I far enough ahead that he didn't get a photo of me? Everyone will know whose blue hair this is."

"I don't think he had time to get anything," Isaiah said, but inside he wasn't so sure.

"I'd better change colors tonight," she said.

"Guess we'll have to sleep on what to do next," Magda said. She twisted her hair into a ponytail, a gesture she seemed to use when she was worried. "Waiting for the dream," she sang, her voice quivering. "Just trying to break the mood."

Isaiah felt a sense of fear crackling through him. "Wind. Jeremiah. Griz. Eagle. All of you! We need your help to stay safe. I hope you're here protecting us." A breeze lifted his bangs and gently put them back down.

Chapter 10

Fire

Eagle guided them inside a crystal cavern where a campfire was burning in the center. The fire reminded Isaiah of the first dream when they had all been sitting around a campfire, but that had been in a forest. The cave was large enough to hold the kids and their animals comfortably. There were rock benches along the walls and rocks to sit on closer to the fire. The floor was smooth white granite that was shiny enough to reflect the dancing flames which were strong and high.

Magda surprised them by saying, "Welcome to the Cave of Healing."

"How do you know it's called the Cave of Healing?" Rose asked.

"I'm not sure," Magda said. "I just had a feeling that was the name. Look at all the different colors of crystals embedded in the walls." The fire's light made the colors dance like tiny rainbow spirals all around them. Isaiah was transfixed by these moving circles, holding up his hands and arms for them to dance over.

Magda moved closer to the fire, lying down beside it. Panther stretched out beside her. "The floor kind of vibrates. There's a hum maybe, and it's moving through my whole body." Yellow and red flames leapt higher and color spiraled across her.

Isaiah lay down in the arms of Grizzly. "I feel the hum, Magda. And my lungs feel very, very hot like the sun is shining in them. It feels really good." He imagined breathing in the tiny, dancing lights, letting their happy joy fill his lungs too. His breathing sounded like music to him. Music that began to hum along with the vibrating floor. He felt so good.

"That's the way I feel when I play soccer. When I am having a good game, a fire grows inside of me stronger and brighter and I feel energized, like I could play all day and never get tired," Magda said.

"I bet the fire could burn up my anger," Rose said. "Of course, that would be one big fire!" She laughed.

"It's kind of like what the wind taught us," Isaiah said. "When we feel sadness, anger, or fear, we can imagine giving the energy to the wind or the fire to be burned up."

"Like to a candle flame or the sun," Rose said.

"Scientifically speaking," George said from across the cavern where Octopus was sheltered from the heat, "fire is very necessary for the earth. Some seeds need the heat of the fire to germinate."

There was a silence as Fire brought more heat to the cave.

Finally, Rose asked, "I wonder what those men are burning behind the warehouse?"

The fire's flames rose higher and higher, flickering against the crystals, touching them.

Magda began coughing. "It's some type of poison. I just feel it."

"I know Eagle guided us here for a reason," said George. "I wonder how Fire can help?"

"Maybe it can help by refusing to burn," Magda said getting up.

"Maybe it can burn back on itself so it doesn't spread," George said. "That's what the firefighters do to stop forest fires."

"So Fire can help us by not burning whatever's in that firepit," Isaiah said.

"I get a hit in my belly that the Fire understands us, and it will help." Magda and Panther left the cave.

The others thanked the fire and followed her. Isaiah was the last one out, not wanting the way he felt to stop. As he turned to say goodbye to the fire, Eagle flew down, retrieved an ember from the fire, and tucked it into Isaiah's chest. It didn't burn at all, but he noticed that the good feeling continued long after he had returned to his bed.

Chapter 11

What is next?

Isaiah opened the lunch gathering beside the pond, "I don't see any smoke so Fire must be helping."

"And there aren't any birds flying around here," George added.

"So we heard the men say they had to dump six barrels a day, and they're going to plow the pond under next week. Today's Friday! They're going to catch on pretty soon that the barrel isn't draining," Isaiah said.

"Next week it may not be safe for us to meet here at the pond because they might be plowing it under," Rose said. "And we can't go back inside the fence to check because they're probably watching for us after yesterday. Sorry, guys."

"It's not your fault, Rose," Isaiah said.

"That's a first," she said, laughing.

"I don't feel safe here," Magda said. "It only makes sense the man thinks we're from the middle school. What if he comes through the gate looking for us? And my soccer team is wondering where I'm going every lunch. I'll be back." She took off running toward the gate.

As Isaiah watched her piling rocks on this side of the gate, he thought, *Magda would be missed by her friends while the rest of us wouldn't be.* When she returned, he said, "I think we need to ask our power animals this weekend in our dreams what we should do."

"We also have to finish our individual animal research so we can start the PowerPoint on Monday," Magda added. "Hash tag homework."

Isaiah thought it felt strange to have her mix school with what they were doing here.

The others looked at her and nodded.

"Our animals know a lot about living a good life," George said. "I think they might have special powers to fix this."

"Without us getting in trouble," Rose added, picking at her purple nail polish on her pinkie finger.

"Right now I think we should bury these birds," Isaiah said taking some gloves from his pocket. "Let's use sticks to make a hole in the earth."

"Before we move anything, we have to document our evidence," George said, phone in hand. He took a close-up of a blackbird.

"Great thinking, George," Magda said, pulling out her phone. "We need to be sure the school is in some of the pictures of the area and the warehouse too."

"And we need pictures of the pond to prove it existed," Rose insisted.

"Rose, you do great diagrams," George said. "Will you sketch the area and label where everything is? Here's my log book where I've been listing the dates and the things that have happened."

Rose took the notebook and leafed through it. She noticed that he'd taped in the diagram she had drawn of the barrel operation. "George, this is brilliant! What made you think of it?"

"I told you I want to be a scientist. Scientists keep log books. Rose, here's my dad's tape measure."

While George and Rose worked making measurements to place on the diagram, Magda took pictures. Isaiah went to work with a long stick scrapping out a giant hole next to the cottonwoods. Soon Magda came to help him which made the hole deepen more quickly.

Diagram complete, Rose laid a large trash bag on the ground, and she and George began placing dead birds on it. When it was full, they pulled it to the hole and slid the birds gently into their grave. A cloud covered the sun. Magda and Isaiah brought another group. The silence was profound. No birds were calling.

No wind. Quiet stillness for six loads of dead birds. Isaiah brought the one with the eagle feather covering it to place last in the hole. As they looked down at the heap of dead blackbirds, the sun came out again, and Eagle flew over, his shadow stroking the burial site.

"There were 109 dead birds." Rose broke the silence. "109! Those stupid idiots!"

"I've got it documented. 109." George said. "I've also collected some of the pond water for science. Don't worry, Rose. I won't tell specifically where it came from."

"What if the toxins in it blow up the science lab?" Magda asked.

"I'll be careful," George said, dropping it into a plastic bag.

They covered the birds with leaves, pinecones and needles and placed a cairn of rocks on the spot. A tombstone. George measured the distances from the trees beside the pit and wrote them in his log book. "In case we need to dig them up later."

The four stood in silence again until the bell sounded on the other side of the cottonwoods. In the distance, a black Labrador watched them.

Isaiah noticed tree branches swept against them as the kids slipped back into the school yard. *Kind of like a pat on the back*, he thought.

That afternoon, their science teacher announced they'd be doing the water tests today. "Part of your lab work will be deciding if we are looking at a physical reaction or a chemical reaction. Okay, in our area, we have to watch for high levels of nitrates in the water from the fertilizers used in farming. Drinking water high in nitrates can interfere with your red blood cells' ability to transport oxygen. This is especially harmful to infants.

"If you brought tap water from your house that is on the city water system, raise your hand. Okay. That's a majority. The nitrate level in city water is regulated and monitored, so we will just check your water against the report they published. Use these test strips.

"If you brought a sample from home and are on well water, raise your hand please," their teacher said. Seven students had their hands up. "We'll also be checking that water for nitrate levels. The kits for that are on the cart. Does anyone have a sample that is from something other than home?"

George alone raised his hand, and Rose choked. "I found this in a pond," he said. "I don't know if we'll find nitrates in it."

"Great," the teacher said. "We probably will because of run-off, but we'll see. We will be sending that sample out to a professional lab to be checked for other chemicals as well. It'll take about ten days. Put it up here on my desk. Okay everyone, partner up and get your supplies."

As he passed George, Isaiah heard Rose say to him, "You'd better know what you're doing."

Chapter 12

Advice

In the Friday night dream, Eagle brought the kids to their power animals around a fire again. This time it was on a canyon floor, and they were surrounded by smooth rock walls that rose all the way to the stars. Looking up was like viewing the sky through a telescope.

"So," George said, "chain reactions. The toxic waste put into the water killed the fish."

"And this will hurt the bears and raccoons who eat the fish," cried Rose.

"Exactly," nodded George. "Everything affects everything else."

"Burning those pellets," said Rose, "made Isaiah's asthma bad and most likely isn't good for anyone's lungs."

"Did eating those pellets kill the birds?" Magda asked.

George sighed. "Those men were probably burning them to dispose of them, spilling them all over the ground, and the birds thought they were food."

"So what do we do now?" Rose asked. "It has already been a whole week!"

Isaiah was lying on his back, looking up at the stars. He loved watching them blink and flash. He noticed there seemed to be a bridge of light linking one side of the canyon with the other. "Look at how the stars connect both rock walls," he whispered.

"Let's go cross that bridge," Rose said, rising up on Giraffe's back.

Magda and Panther were already halfway across the bridge of stars when the others got there. "This is so cool," she said. "Come on!"

Rose stopped beside Magda. "Look," she said.

Isaiah followed her pointing finger.

Across the dark sky, letters appeared to form out of the stars. "Follow the ancient ways," they said.

"What does that mean?" Isaiah asked.

George said, "The ancient people had abilities that modern science cannot explain like how they lifted the final blocks into the pyramids or cut the crop circles so perfectly without being able to see them from above."

"So does this mean that ancient people would know how to get rid of these toxins that weren't even invented when they were around?" Magda asked.

"It probably means they had a way of accessing information that we need to find out about," George said.

Magda said, "I just wish there was some way to get advice from our animals during the day. It's hard having to wait to go to sleep every night before we are in touch, although I do feel Panther with me all the time." She patted Panther.

"Hey!" Isaiah said as Magda's question nudged something to land solidly in his mind. "That's it! We're waiting to meet in our dreams to go places to learn things. What if there's a way to speak to our animals in the middle of the day?"

He felt a grizzly hugging him.

"I think we can," Rose said, "I've heard about a technique ancient peoples used to talk to plants to find out how to use them or to travel ahead to find out what weather was coming toward them."

Isaiah felt excitement rising in him. "Tomorrow's Saturday. Can everyone meet at the pond?" His mother was working so he'd be free to go without questions. "I bet we can figure this out," Isaiah said.

"I have soccer practice in the morning, but afternoon works for me," Magda said.

The others were available in the afternoon too, so the plan was set.

"It's called a shamanic journey," George said, pointing to the new arrangement of stars.

Chapter 13

Journeying

"I had the whole morning to look on the Internet about what we're trying to do," George said. "This ancient shamanic practice called journeying, well, people still do it. I found a website that had instructions."

"Do your instructions look like this?" Isaiah asked, showing George a printout of what he had found on the Internet. The boys laughed. They had been on the same website.

"As they say, great minds think alike!" Isaiah said as he high-fived George.

Isaiah read from his notes: *"Many enter into the Hidden Worlds through dreams, but there is a way to enter these worlds via performing a special ceremony called journeying."*

"When you journey into the Hidden Worlds, you travel outside of time where all the spirits (for example: animals, birds, insects, reptiles, plants, trees, and rocks) who want to help can speak to you, advise you, and teach you," Isaiah read. "Hey! We've already spoken to Jeremiah, Wind and Fire in our dreams, and they all helped us."

"And we have our own power animals," Magda said.

"And Eagle who leads us places," Rose added.

"Right!" Isaiah continued, *"Once upon a time all humankind could see and communicate with these spirits. Then when science became strong, people started trusting only what they could see with their eyes, feel with their hands, hear with their ears, and smell and taste physically. A veil formed between the worlds.*

"Soon only special people called shamans could see and speak with the spirits. And they became the people who could help their communities in working with the invisible helping-spirits."

The others listened carefully as Isaiah continued, *"In the Hidden Worlds there are three levels: the Lower World, the Middle*

World, and the Upper World. The Middle World is where we live. The Lower World has forests, jungles, oceans, beaches, and deserts. All the landscapes we have in our world exist there. The Upper World is the place of the sky. In either world, there are many landscapes to travel to and many helping-spirits in many forms."

"This is interesting," George said. "If these worlds exist outside of time and space, we aren't on the clock when we visit Lower World or Upper World. *'Being there for a few minutes could seem like hours and days in the Hidden Realms.'* That makes total sense because it seemed like our visit to Jeremiah took all night— but it probably didn't since people dream a lot in one night."

"I think all we have to do is close our eyes and go into our imagination," Isaiah said. "It should work." He kept reading. *"When you journey, you should set an intention or have a guiding question.* I guess we all know what that is," he said to the group. "What is our next step with the warehouse situation?"

George nodded and continued, *"To get to Lower World, you must travel down. To do this, locate a way to go deeper into the earth (for example: through a hole, a tree trunk, a cave, a volcano, or a body of water you can swim through).* Well, we already know we can make our bodies smaller to go into these openings since in these dreams our bodies don't have limitations."

"I think we need to take our Power Animals with us," Magda said.

"Great idea," said Isaiah. "I want to try going down through water like George did with Jeremiah. I'm going to imagine my reflection on the surface of the water and then dive through it."

"Water's very cool," George assured him. "because you can breathe in the water as you move through it. Your asthma won't be a problem."

"I'm going through some tree roots I saw once on a camping trip. They were all twisty and you could see a tiny opening at the base of the pine tree," Magda said. She waved, called to Panther, and closed her eyes to enter the tunnel.

"I want to try a cave," George said.

"I'm diving into a volcano," Rose said. "I'm off to Lower World to find out our next step!"

Isaiah lay back on the ground, closed his eyes, and imagined himself diving into a large, clear lake. Grizzly was right beside him.

Chapter 14

Lower World Travels

The four of them and their animals met up in a meadow filled with tall, green grass and wild flowers of blue, yellow, and pink. The flowers were waving, welcoming them.

"So this is Lower World," Isaiah said looking around.

"How do you like the water?" George asked.

"I could breathe in it just like you said, George. I asked how, and the water told me that it is a living being too. Babies breathe in water before they're born so it makes sense. It was cleansing and purifying me while I swam. It told me I should honor water whenever I take a bath or drink it. It talked to me in my head, and I could hear it! Just like Rose hears."

"Very cool! I guess the water didn't have time to teach me all of that when I was with Jeremiah turning off the valve," George said.

"Probably not," Isaiah agreed. "What happened to you on your way here?"

"A beautiful woman who was dressed in this long, green gown came out of the cave. Emerald light was shining through her. She said she was the spirit of earth," George said.

"Did she say anything else?" Isaiah asked George.

"She had me think a thought, any thought. So I thought about how lucky I was to be traveling through a cave to Lower World. The second I thought it, I saw my words ripple through this shimmering web touching everything connected to it. Words sure have a lot of power. I really need to be careful about what I think and say."

"That's true!" Magda said. "When I came out of the long tunnel of tree roots, I talked to some spirits too. I actually saw them come out of the rocks where they live. They were elves, gnomes, and fairies. I used to think they were make-believe, but today I saw them! I was able to see like all of you do! They welcomed me to their earth garden and *told me that they take care of the earth. They said speaking words is like planting seeds. Something grows out of every word we speak. Our lives are like gardens, and we get to choose what grows in them based on the words we plant."*

"I just wonder what the gardens look like for those men killing the fish?" Rose muttered.

"Good question," Isaiah agreed. "Did you talk to anyone, Rose?"

"I talked to Volcano," she said, "about how some see her as destructive, but she's always clearing things so change can happen. We talked about how anger erupts like a volcano and how it can destroy or be a force for change. Giraffe told me that I can learn to channel my anger into doing good things like stopping the poisons from killing the birds and fish."

Isaiah nodded. "We've each received important information. Let's go back and talk about it. Retrace your exact steps that you took getting here. I'll go back through the water. George re-enter your cave. Rose, you go back through the volcano and Magda through the tree roots."

As if on cue, the animals lifted them and like a flash moving outside of time, they were magically transported back the way they'd come.

Chapter 15

Ideas

"Okay, so one idea is that we need to honor the water by getting it cleaned up so it can continue its important healing work," Isaiah said.

"And we need to watch our thinking about the situation so we don't make it worse," said George.

Magda added, "Yeah, we need to plant seeds of hope, seeds of knowing that all of this damage can be fixed."

Rose said, "Well, I'm mad enough about it that if I just send a little of my anger into fixing it, it'll help a lot." She laughed, and her magenta hair and nails (today's colors) seemed to vibrate.

"So we know what needs to happen. Any ideas for where to start?" Isaiah asked.

"We've already got a water specimen being tested in a professional lab," George reminded them. He looked at Rose.

"My mom's on the city council," Magda contributed.

"I forgot about that!" George shouted.

"Me too," Isaiah said. "We could tell your mom."

"Or we could ask her if we can speak to the whole group," Magda added.

"I think we still need more facts before we tell any adults," Rose said. "We have to make a detailed plan, including what we know for certain and how we know it. George's log book is a super start, but we need to gather more information. Most important though, we need to be sure we're not incriminating ourselves."

"One of my sisters is on the youth city council," George said. "Maybe we should ask her or some other high school kids to help us."

"Whatever we decide, we need to act fast," Rose reminded

them. "It won't take long for them to discover the valve has been turned off. Like I said before, it's already been a week!"

"This week they might plow the pond under," Magda said. She slapped her forehead. "We could tell my Uncle Robb what those men are doing."

"What if the dumping was his idea?" George asked. "It's very expensive to clean up poison. When he's not talking sports, my dad talks about the bottom line and how important it is to make the big bucks."

"We don't know who's involved, so we have to be very careful," Isaiah said. "Hey, do you see that black lab out there? It's like he's watching us. He might be the same one I saw at the warehouse."

"He looks hungry," Rose said. "And abandoned." She walked toward the dog. "Here boy." The dog took off running in the opposite direction. Rose sat back down.

Magda said, "I don't think my Uncle Robb's involved, but okay. We could do a letter writing campaign."

"Right!" Rose said. "We could do it anonymously. We could even put a letter in the paper."

"We could make posters about possible toxic waste in our town," Magda said. "I make them for my soccer team all the time."

"Easy for you to say. You aren't the one the man saw. We have to be really careful. What if he sees us hanging the posters?" Rose asked. "And what if he figures out the posters are about the warehouse? It won't take him long to figure out where the information came from. I don't like this. I don't like this at all."

Isaiah gave her a reassuring pat. "We won't choose any ideas that'll put any of us in danger. We're just brainstorming right now."

"Okay," Rose said.

Isaiah continued, "My mom said the radio station at the college did the piece on this new business. We could send the radio station a bunch of questions and ask them to do a follow up."

"My oldest sister goes to the college. I bet she has friends at the radio station," George said. "Hey! Wait! Cause and Effect. What if we ask the teachers to set up a field trip so we can learn how this company disposes of poison waste so it doesn't have a lasting effect on the environment? They couldn't just lie to a bunch of teachers and the parent sponsors and the whole seventh grade."

"And we could invite my mom to be a sponsor on the field trip so she'd hear what they say. Maybe she or my dad could set up the field trip with Uncle Robb," Magda said.

"Isaiah, your mom works at the college, doesn't she? Maybe she knows someone there who could test the birds and fish for poison," Rose said.

"I don't want to worry her. She worries a lot," Isaiah said. He thought about how upset his mother would be if she knew what he was involved in. "Maybe we could do all the other ideas."

"With help, we've done some temporary stops. I think now we need to find an agency to help us," George said, "so the correct adults can handle this with the laws that are in place." He wiped his glasses. "And that way we won't be outrunning mad men anymore." He nodded at Rose. "Hey, the dog is back." They all watched the dog, tail between its legs, moving carefully toward them. Isaiah began making kissing sounds. The dog lay down. He moved toward the dog. The dog watched but didn't move. He put out his hand, talking quietly to the dog. The dog lifted its head and sniffed. Then he began petting it. The others gathered around.

"It's a female, and she's recently had a litter of pups. Probably still nursing them," George said. "Are you hungry, girl?"

"She looks half starved," Magda said.

"Where are your puppies?" Rose asked. She sat down and put the dog's head in her lap. "George, if I give you money, will you go and get some dog food for her? I'll wait with her here."

"I have to get home," Magda said. "Don't forget to do your PowerPoint homework. Isaiah, do you need a ride?"

They left Rose talking softly to the dog while George headed for the store.

Chapter 16

Organizing

It was after three when Isaiah got home. He got right to work on his research about grizzly bears. His mom would be home at 5:30 p.m. and the pizza would be there at 6. He had to hurry with his homework. He had spent the morning doing his chores and the research on journeying, skipping his video games. He was surprised that he didn't really miss his usual ritual. Maybe this is what growing up felt like. Making different choices. But he also hadn't done his homework. He hoped he had enough time now.

For his research, he was looking for causes and effects of the environment on grizzlies and of grizzlies on the environment. He found out that the San Juan Mountains of Colorado used to have a large grizzly population but killing by ranchers and the government depleted the population. The last grizzly was found in 1979. There were reports that another was sighted in 1989, but without proof, the grizzly is still listed as extinct in Colorado. He learned that grizzlies are important to the ecosystem because they excrete the seeds from the fruit they eat which plants more fruit. Also, they stir up the soil when foraging for bulbs, tree roots and squirrels which brings up nitrogen for the environment. Hadn't his science teacher talked about nitrogen being essential to life but that too much of it in the water was bad? And they had used ammonium nitrate to make those cold packs. He guessed what grizzlies did was a good thing. He kept going until he had twenty cause-effect details. Just as he finished, he heard his mom's car pulling into the garage. Whew!

In the middle of a heated Monopoly game on Sunday afternoon, the phone rang. Isaiah's mother looked at him as she handed him the phone. He knew she was thinking something was up. He'd had so few calls from friends in his life.

"Isaiah!" George yelled. "We've got trouble."

"What's up?" Isaiah asked, moving away from his mom, worried she might be able to hear George.

"Remember Tuesday when my foot slipped into the pond?"

"Uh-huh."

"Well, I got worried that whatever was in that fish-killing water might be bad for my foot, so I didn't want to take any chances. I threw my shoes away. And my mom figured out my shoes are missing!"

"What'd she say?" Isaiah asked. His mother came around the corner when he said 'she'. He shrugged at her like it was no big deal.

"She was really mad and yelled about how they were new for school this year and how I don't appreciate the money they cost and how she spent hours searching for them when she hadn't seen me wearing them and blah, blah, blah. I told her I accidently slipped into a stream with dead fish, and it was disgusting. All true. I just skipped the part about toxic poisons. Anyway, I'm grounded for two weeks. And I have to pay her back for the shoes. That part is no problem, but if we need to meet anywhere other than school or dream time, I'm out."

"That stinks," Isaiah said. "But we'll work it out." He didn't want to say anything more that might tip off his mother. "Did you get the groceries?"

"Oh, dog food? Yes, we fed her. She was really hungry. After she ate, she headed back toward the field behind the warehouse. We think she must be living there. We tried to follow but lost her. I just hope she and the puppies are safe."

"Me too. Thanks for letting me know." They disconnected.

"George. From school. From my group project," Isaiah said to his mother as he headed back to the game. "He handled a problem we ran into."

His mother followed. The less he said, the better.

At lunch on Monday, George brought a flow chart in his log book. "Rose helped me do this before school."

Rose showed the group, her purple nails tracing along the boxes. Box one said:"109 dead red-winged blackbirds by the pond. Many dead fish in the stream that feeds the pond and in the pond too."

There was an arrow from box 1 to box 2. "Barrels draining into the stream (skull and crossbones on barrels)," with an arrow to box 3: "Valve closed so draining can't happen but we did it during lunch=trespassing!"

The second row of boxes and arrows followed this sequence: "Overheard 3 men talking about 6 barrels per week and plowing under the pond." Next: "We were trespassing during lunch when we were off school grounds!" The final box in this row said, "We are so busted if we tell about this!"

Row 3 went from "Bag of pellets beside a smoking fire pit with 'Avi' on the side. Also said 'proved to cull blackbirds'. Caution sign." to "The birds were eating the pellets and dying." to "Trespassing again!"

"I think we have some dead ends to deal with," she said. "But I'm ready to channel my anger like Volcano said and do something about this."

Isaiah had brought a list of their ideas from the campfire. He'd made it into a chart as well which he shared with the group and then handed to George to paste into his log book. The list was in three columns. The first column was the idea. Column two said, "Should we do it? Yes or No." The third column was the person in charge.

- Water test sent to professional lab — done — George
- Talk to Magda's mom so she can tell the city council — maybe — Magda
- Talk to the city council — ? — Magda
- Get more facts/do research — yes — ?

- Make a plan—Yes—?
- Talk to George's sister and the youth council for advice—?—George
- Talk to Magda's Uncle Robb—No—Magda
- Do an anonymous letter writing campaign—?—?
- Write an anonymous letter to the newspaper—?—?
- Make posters and put them up at night—maybe—Magda
- Send questions to the college radio station—maybe—George
- Take a field trip to the new company and invite Magda's mom to be a sponsor—maybe—Magda
- Ask Isaiah's mom if she knows someone at the college who could test the birds—Absolutely not!—Isaiah
- Find an agency—yes—?

"We talked about a lot of things, but George suggested we find an agency and that sounds to me like the best way to go about this," Isaiah said.

"What kind of agency, George?" Rose asked.

"Maybe there's an agency in charge of water, air and hazardous waste," George suggested. "Towns usually have them."

"I wonder if we have one or if we're too small?" Rose said.

"We have time in the computer lab this afternoon," Magda reminded them. "If we get our PowerPoint done really fast, we can research it."

Rose looked at George. "I'll help you so you get your work done faster."

George smiled at her. "Thank you."

"You should ask Octopus to help too. With all of her fingers, you would get done really fast!" Magda laughed.

"Let's do a quick journey to get ideas for what kind of agency," Isaiah said. He smiled at the thought that already it seemed normal to journey to these Hidden Worlds.

Chapter 17

The Agency

They looked at each other and closed their eyes. Isaiah noticed that the pine needles beneath him were fragrant as he took in deep breaths of air. The sun warmed and comforted him. He felt his heartbeat merging with the beating in the ground. *What an incredible feeling,* he thought. He found his reflection in the pond, saw Grizzly beside him, and Dove.

When they were all in the meadow, Magda said, "I think we were linked telepathically. I felt all of you becoming the earth. I could feel all of us being warmed by the sun. I could smell the pine needles and felt like everyone was smelling them at the same time. It was so peaceful. It was like I was inside of all of you!"

The others nodded, knowing exactly what she meant. A black stallion came out of the meadow. Eagle was riding on him. The horse came right up to the group and stood whinnying. He did not speak, but his actions said, "Welcome!" He started swaying his head and body in such a way that it showed he wanted everyone to follow him.

The kids jumped on their power animals so that they could keep up with the stallion who took off at a fast speed.

They ran through the meadow to a circle of trees. Once there, the stallion stopped and stood there like he would wait for them on the outside of the trees. Eagle flew into the circle, and the kids followed with their power animals. Each sat down with his/her back against a tree. George said, "I can see the roots of this tree and the roots of all of your trees."

"It must be the web," Rose said. "I can see roots shooting out of the bottom of my feet and down into the earth!"

"Me too," Magda said smiling. "I hope they won't slow down my running!"

Isaiah cleared his throat. "Let's connect roots and ask what kind of agency we need to find."

While they hooked roots, the trees began to sway and hum. They wove their branches in and through each other. Isaiah noticed that they were forming a large ball that extended beneath and above them. He felt rocked, as if their humming were a lullaby.

Isaiah felt water washing over him. He felt refreshed, recharged. He looked at the others. There was water dripping from Magda's hair. Rose's fluorescent pink hair was washed backwards and George was wiping his face. Everyone had been washed.

He closed his eyes and focused on their question again. What do we need to know about an agency? *A breeze came out of the trees, drying Isaiah off. And then he saw in his mind row after row of barrels, lines and lines of barrels. Each barrel was vibrating, the skull and crossbones gyrating.*

And just like that the journey was over. The trees pulled back, unwinding their roots and branches. Eagle left the clearing. The stallion pawed the ground and shook his head. Grizzly picked up Isaiah and carried him from the clearing. George, flying on the back of Octopus, came behind him. Rose and Giraffe followed George, and Magda, on the back of Panther, brought up the end. Once again they flew behind the stallion to the meadow.

At the pond, Isaiah sat up and looked around him. "So what did that mean?" he asked the others. "We got wet and then I felt wind and saw lines of dancing barrels."

"That's what I saw!" the other three said in unison.

"Okay," said Isaiah. "We all got the same information. What is the answer? What agency?"

George started to laugh. "Really?!?" he said and slapped his thigh.

"What?" Rose demanded.

"Don't you get it?" George asked still laughing.

"Get what?" Isaiah asked.

"Water. Air. Toxic wastes." George counted off on three fingers.

"Yes, I got that," Rose said. "We all did. What does it mean?"

"Oh!" Isaiah started laughing as well. "We asked what agency? The agency of water, air and toxic wastes," he said.

"OH!" Magda and Rose said in unison.

George said, "Like I said before we journeyed."

Isaiah said, "Magda's idea is good — we use our computer lab time to find out if that agency is here in town and if so, where. Hopefully we'll find out what their rules are. Maybe we can go there and tell them what we know. And we can show them the pictures and George's log book."

"And let them know they have to keep it a secret about how we know. I've told you before, I don't want to get in trouble for going off the school grounds and for trespassing. My parents would ground me for the rest of my life. And I hate being home alone," Rose said. She looked at them one by one and added, "Although lately I haven't felt so lonely."

George looked at Isaiah. "I know what you mean about getting grounded."

"Remember: This is the week the pond gets plowed under!" Magda warned. "Hash tag: Pond Going Under."

"Let's take it one step at a time," Isaiah said. "Let's pass any information we get around to each other in the lab."

Chapter 18

The Law

Magda finished with typing her cause-effect information on panther first and started the note in the computer lab. She wrote: *I found lots of boards and commissions and stuff I don't understand listed for our town, but it doesn't look like we have one agency for air, water, and hazardous materials.*

Isaiah added, *I found the same thing. There's some 234-page booklet, but it looks complicated. I clicked on something else that took me to the State of Colorado.*

George is almost done. I'm helping him. Then we'll start looking. Rose wrote back.

Awhile later, Magda got up and went to the printer and then to the stapler. She gave the thumbs up to the group. A few minutes passed and then two pages came around from the State of Colorado website. The top said, 'Reporting Environmental Spills'. Under a section about clean water, she underlined *'a release of any toxic substance entering Colorado water must be reported immediately'*. She had double underlined *immediately*. *What do we do now? Are we in trouble because we've known a whole, entire week?* Magda had written.

Isaiah read her notations and then looked at the section about clean air. He wrote: *We don't know for sure if what they're putting in the water is hazardous, and we don't know what they're burning, and we don't know what kind of permit they have or what they are allowed to do by law since they are a company that disposes hazardous waste.*

George wrote: *Right, but we still need to tell someone who can look at what they're doing and see if it's okay. I don't think the fish and the birds would die if they were doing things the right way.*

Magda added: *I found a 24-Hour Reporting Hotline. It's an 800 number. Should we make an anonymous call?*

Rose wrote: *OMG! What if they find out who is calling? They're going to know we were trespassing. During lunch. Off of school grounds. And this could destroy their business. They'll be mad. The man saw what I looked like and not everyone in this school puts wild colors in their hair, may I remind you? I am the target here. OMG!*

What if my Uncle Robb is somehow involved? Magda wrote. *What if he's our target?*

The teacher announced, "Five minutes, folks. Start to shut down."

Isaiah's heart was racing. He took some deep breaths. Rose had a good point. But they had to do something. The fish and birds were dying. The water and air were being polluted. Other animals and humans would be affected. The group was waiting for him to make a decision. How had he become the leader anyway? *Grizzly, help! What should I tell them?* He thought with desperation.

He heard Grizzly whisper, "The agency will help. You can trust them. The birds are buried by the cottonwood trees which is on school property."

Isaiah signaled to the others to meet him by the copy machine as the class began lining up. "Grizzly said the agency can be trusted to help us, and Rose, the birds are buried on school grounds."

Rose sighed deeply.

"Let's meet up in dream time and make our plan so that our animals can help us," he said as the class filed down the hall.

Chapter 19

The Plan

That night when Isaiah got to dream time, George was waiting for him. "Hurry! There's something they have to show us at the school."

Isaiah grabbed onto Grizzly and followed George. The girls were hovering above the school, shimmering in the starlight. It was cold in reality, but here he couldn't even see their breath.

Magda pointed, and he realized he could see through the roof of the building. Isaiah followed her finger. The night janitor was cleaning the main office. Then they watched as he went through the school, checking to be sure all the doors were locked.

"This is the same pattern he follows every night," Octopus said. "Never deviates."

"Panther agrees," Magda said. "Notice that he unlocks, cleans, and relocks every door. He goes to each classroom and every office starting at the cafeteria." Her finger traced his route through the school.

Finally, the janitor stepped into a small room off of the main office. There were TV screens on the wall and a computer.

"What's he doing now?" asked Rose.

"Turning the cameras back on and setting the security system," said George.

"The cameras are turned off around 3:00 in the afternoon when he comes in to work. Guess he doesn't want to be filmed as he unlocks and relocks," said Isaiah. "Notice where the nurse's office is in his cleaning pattern. He does it around 4:00."

The others looked at him. "Why does that matter?" asked Rose.

"Because I have an idea," Isaiah answered. "What if I went to the nurse's office, where there's a phone, saying I felt an asthma attack coming on at the end of eighth period?"

"And you make the call? Without us?" Magda said. "No way!"

"No, we have to make the call together, so keep listening," Isaiah

66

said. "Every time I've been there at the end of the day, the nurse goes down to the office to check her mailbox at about 3:20, right before the bell. I've almost missed my bus a couple of times waiting for her to get back to sign me out."

"Okay," said Rose. "So?"

"So you," Isaiah said to Rose, "have PE eighth period, right? You need to change really fast and leave early. Come to the nurse's office and hide under the bed while the nurse is out. She'll sign me out. I'll leave. As soon as she leaves, you come out from under the bed and let us in."

Isaiah stopped. "Look!" The janitor was circling the building, checking each of the outside doors.

"He's on camera," George said, following the janitor's movements on the TV monitors in the main office.

The janitor got into a black Ram pick-up and drove away.

"So," Rose said to Isaiah. "I get to be the one who could potentially get caught in the nurse's office by a guy who drives a big ass truck? Great. Is that because I'm the one with a record?"

"No," Isaiah told her. "It's because PE is the easiest class to leave early."

"And because Volcano told you to direct your anger into doing good," George added, patting her arm. "This is good."

Rose smiled.

Isaiah continued. "So Rose, you let the three of us into the side door, and we make the call together. The only thing I have to figure out is what to tell my mom about why I'm not taking the bus home."

Rose said, "Tell her our whole group is going to my house to work on our PowerPoint. My parents won't be home. My house is only a couple of blocks away."

"And I'll have my mom pick us up there. She can take you and George home," Magda offered.

"Perfect!" Isaiah said. Then he remembered that George was grounded. "Will this work for you?" he asked him.

"I'm okay if it's for school," George said. He added, "Good thing *the nurse's door is on the side of the building away from the parking lot. That's convenient."*

"Yeah," Rose said, "Magda, you'd better not forget to bring the 24-hour hotline number with you."

"I'll write it on the side of my lucky soccer shoes," Magda said. "They're always with me."

Rose asked the animals. "Will this work?" She paused, tilting her head to the side. "Giraffe just said we can do this. You're right, George. This is good."

Chapter 20

Success—Barely!

Tuesday afternoon Isaiah was lying on the bed in the nurse's office watching the clock. It was 3:30 pm. The bell rang. Where was Rose? She'd better hurry up. What if the nurse got back before she got here?

He heard the outer door open and watched Rose hurry into the room. "Rose, what took so long?" he asked.

"I got busted by my PE teacher. She caught me sneaking out of class early."

Just then the outer door opened again. Rose jumped into the closet, barely getting the door closed before the nurse bustled in.

"Are you okay to ride the bus, Isaiah?" the nurse asked him. "You look pretty pale."

"I'm okay," he said, his voice cracking. Now of all times.

"I can call your mother," she offered.

"No, I'm better. Thank you."

He walked down the hall slowly in case the nurse was still watching. As he turned the corner, he saw George slip out of the main office.

"The cameras are off," George said.

"How'd you...?"

"My case manager sent me down to mail something. I was watching for Rose. She wasn't coming. The bell rang, and the nurse was heading back. Rose owes Magda big time because she stalled the nurse until Rose flew past."

We'd better hurry." They turned the corner and saw Magda tugging on the nurse's outside door.

She saw them. "Come help me. It's stuck."

The three of them tugged while Rose pushed from the inside. Finally it flew open. Isaiah looked around before he slipped in to make sure no one was watching them.

Rose handed the phone to Isaiah.

"Oh no, Rose. You make the call. They'll trust a girl more and won't think it's a prank."

"I want to listen, but I don't know if I can keep from getting mad," Rose said. "You do it," she turned to Magda. "You do great under pressure. I've seen you play soccer."

Magda took the phone and dialed. "Hello, I need to report some possible violations," she said. The others listened as she gave the information about finding the dead birds and fish, telling the person on the other end that she and her friends had been off of the school grounds. "That's why this call has to be anonymous," she explained.

She gave the address of the warehouse and told the location of the buried birds. She spelled the partial name on the bag of pellets and reported what they had done to the valve on the barrel. "The fish were all dead in the pond. We also overheard some men talk about dumping six barrels a day and plowing under the pond this week.

"There's a skull and crossbones on each barrel," she said after a pause. "We have pictures of everything and diagrams in a log book." She wrote down the address of where to mail the evidence.

She had just finished writing the zip code when there was the sound of a key being inserted into the lock on the nurse's door.

"The janitor! He's early!" whispered Rose. "Isaiah and George, get out of here. I'll follow with Magda." He heard the squeak of the janitor's shoes as he entered the outer section of the office. The light went on. She pulled on Magda's arm.

"Ugh. Bye," Magda blurted as she replaced the phone and quickly hurried to where Isaiah was holding the door open.

They hurried down the sidewalk, pelted by large snowflakes. When had it started snowing? It was coming down fast.

"OMG!" Magda said when they got to corner of the building.

"Where's Rose? And look!"

They all looked back at the nurse's door. Three sets of fresh footprints in the snow came out of the nurse's door and down the walk. And there was no Rose! Had she been caught?

"Where is she? She was right behind me," Magda said, "Panther, quick. We need your help. Find Rose."

They watched in amazement as their footprints disappeared and only those of Panther remained. Then he disappeared.

Magda didn't even think. She slipped into journey space and floated above the school like in the dream. She noticed Isaiah and George had the same idea. Rose was in the closet. The janitor emptied the trash, swept under the bed and sprayed the surfaces with cleaner. He tugged on the outside door which wasn't completely closed. The latch clicked as it locked. He went into the other room, sweeping and emptying trash. Then he turned off the lights and locked the door.

Rose popped out of the closet and ran to the outside door. It was stuck again. Magda immediately pulled on it as Rose pushed. The boys came to help, and the door opened. Isaiah made sure he heard it click when he pushed it closed. He also brushed their footprints away. He looked behind to check his work, and there were Panther's prints again, covering theirs.

"That was too close!" Rose said. "I thought I was going to have to spend the night in there!"

"I could smell his after-shave!" Isaiah said, noticing that his hands were shaking, but his breathing was normal. How could that be? And it was really cold outside. Where was his asthma? He felt the ember glowing, the one Grizzly had placed in his chest when they were in the cave.

"Do you think the janitor heard me say goodbye?" Magda asked.

"He was wearing headphones when I saw him turn off the cameras," George said.

"Oh no!" Rose said, stopping in the middle of the walk. "How are we going to know if the hotline people follow up on our complaint?" Rose asked. "Did you get a chance to ask, Magda?"

"No. I ran out of time," Magda answered. "Rose is right. How will we know?"

A horn honked, and they all jumped. It was Magda's mom. "Why weren't you kids waiting for me inside?" she called. "Get in the warm car now."

Apparently Magda's mom hadn't noticed that there were no footprints leading up to Rose's porch, Isaiah thought. *They hadn't made it to her house before their ride arrived. Everything was so close! What else could happen?*

Chapter 21

The Announcement

The intercom came on the next morning during math. "We need all classes to report to the gym immediately," the secretary announced.

"Put your pencils down and line up please," their teacher said.

What could this be about? Isaiah sent a look to George as they walked down the hall.

The principal answered his question as soon as everyone was seated. "Last night we had an intruder in the nurse's office."

Isaiah's breath caught, and he looked quickly at Magda and Rose. Beside him, George gulped.

The principal continued, "Actually it was outside of the nurse's office. The night janitor found the problem when he did his rounds."

Time seemed to stop. *What will my mother say?* Isaiah wondered.

"The intruder was a large cat," he heard the principal saying.

What?

"We've never had this problem before, and we aren't sure why he came up to the nurse's door and not the trash bins out back."

We know, Isaiah thought.

"Anyway, the snow stopped about five o'clock last night, so he had to have been there in the late afternoon. We're having this assembly to let you know that there is a large cat in the area. If you see it, make yourself look really big. Raise your shoulders, wave your arms, and make a lot of noise."

The principal continued on about notifying their parents, but Isaiah wasn't listening. He was trying to slow his heart down, and he was watching that once again in a stressful situation, his asthma hadn't started up. *I wonder why?* he thought.

"I almost wet my pants!" Rose said on their way back to class. "An urge that has happened a lot in the past 24 hours."

"I know what you mean," George said, laughing. "That was intense!"

"I still want to know how we're going to know what the hotline does," Magda said.

"We'll have to watch the warehouse to see when it gets shut down," George said.

"We can also journey," said Isaiah. "Hey, did you all notice that there was no dream last night?"

"You're right," George said. "I wonder if we're done sharing dreams?"

"We'll have to wait and see, I guess," said Isaiah.

Chapter 22

Watch

In language arts, they only had time to decide on their PowerPoint design and format, and then they each worked on their particular animal slides.

At lunch, Rose asked, "So what's next?" She sat on the log beside the pond. Today the smell was less intense. Either that or they were getting used to it.

"To start, we have to mail the evidence," Magda said.

"I can do that tonight after school," Rose volunteered. "George, I'll need the log book and pictures." She smiled at George. "I will stop at my parents' office first and make a photocopy of everything. Want to come?"

"Sorry I can't. I'm grounded. Long story. Like I said before, we have to watch the warehouse," George said.

They were all looking at Isaiah. "We have to be careful," Isaiah said.

"You're right. People are wondering why we look at each other so much and stuff," Magda said.

Once more Isaiah found himself thinking about what it must be like to be popular. To have people notice what you are doing and who you are looking at.

"We should probably stop meeting at every lunch," Magda said. "So no one thinks anything."

"Okay," Isaiah said. He looked at George and Rose and wondered if they were feeling as let down as he was about the thought of this group disbanding. It had only been a week and a half, but it had been really nice having friends during lunch and someone to share an adventure with. *The adventure isn't over yet,* he thought. *Not until the warehouse is shut down.* And they were still a group in language arts. "I think George is right. We have to keep tabs, so what about if we each take a week? Once a day the person who is on duty will slip over here at lunch and look around."

Isaiah continued, "We have to be really careful not to be seen so stay in the trees and scope out the pond first to see if it has been plowed under. Then stay in the tree line, move toward the fence and listen and look."

"Whoever does that can watch for the dog. I've been feeding her every night," Rose said.

"Nice, Rose." George smiled at her. "I'll bring my binoculars, and we can hide them out here."

"Great idea, George," Isaiah said. "Do you want to take the first watch starting tomorrow?"

"Okay. I'll take tomorrow and Friday. Then I'll do next week too. Maybe they'll jump right on it, and I'll be the only one who'll have to watch," George said.

"Fat chance!" Rose snorted. "We're dealing with bureaucracy. It'll probably take weeks."

"It can't!" Magda shouted. "Hash tag HurryUp! Hash tag Animals Dying!"

Rose patted her on the arm. "I'm sorry. I'm probably wrong."

Isaiah flashed on the fight the two had recently. Things were really shifting between them.

Magda pulled out her phone. "Let's trade numbers so we can shoot texts."

"I don't have a smart phone," Isaiah said. His mother didn't even have one. She thought the extra expense was unnecessary.

"That rules out text messages then." Magda sighed.

"It's probably better not to have anything to trace," Rose responded, patting Isaiah's back. "Besides we're not allowed to use them in school, and I'd probably get caught. That's why I don't even turn mine on at school."

Isaiah smiled at Rose in gratitude.

"How about a sign of some sort?" George suggested. "Like a

yellow ribbon? I'll tie a yellow ribbon on this tree right here." He pulled down a branch.

"Good. We can see that from the school yard," Isaiah said.

"What does the ribbon mean?" Rose asked.

"Oh yeah," George said. "Details." They all laughed. "Yellow ribbon means no sign yet. We're still waiting."

"So the day the ribbon is gone means we've kicked some serious butt!" Rose kicked at a pile of branches.

"Who's next on watch?" Magda asked. She had opened her phone calendar.

Isaiah thought, *She has a schedule that is bigger than my school-home-school schedule.*

"I'll go," Rose volunteered.

"I'll be third," Isaiah said thinking that if the agency got right on it, Magda would never have to leave her 'people' during lunch.

"Thanks, Isaiah," Magda said smiling at him.

Rose said, "Now remember: if one of us gets caught, we keep the rest of us out of it."

George clapped his hands. "That will be our rotation then. Octopus-Giraffe-Bear-Panther." George chanted, "Octo-Gira-Bear and Pant. Try it," he said. "It's a memory technique."

"Octo-Gira-Bear and Pant," the others chanted.

Rose added, "'Ribbon up. Nothin' doin'. It goes down. Trouble brewin'.'"

Laughing and chanting, they sneaked one at a time back onto the school grounds and dispersed.

Chapter 23

Scare

Isaiah awoke Thursday morning and realized there had been no dream for the four of them again. It made him feel lonely in a new way. Before he hadn't had friends to miss.

At the end of lunch, he saw a yellow ribbon waving from the branch George had selected yesterday. In a way he felt sad that the agency hadn't done anything yet, but he reminded himself that they had just made the call two days before. He noticed that Rose was looking across the school yard at him. She nodded at the ribbon, and he gave her a thumbs-up. She shook her head and did a thumbs-down. He laughed.

He saw George just as he slipped out of the cottonwoods. He saw Isaiah and smiled.

Isaiah looked out at the soccer field where Magda and her people were running up and down. He saw her stop for just one second as she noticed the ribbon. Then she dove back into the game. *I wonder if she misses us,* Isaiah thought.

Friday the ribbon was still there. And it was their group's turn to present their PowerPoint. Naturally Magda started them off and then each of them presented their particular animals, in alphabetical order. Isaiah did the conclusion. He was very surprised at how easy it was for him to speak in front of the class. In the past that had been the very worst thing he ever had to do. This time, with the three of them standing by him, he flowed through his parts, and his voice didn't crack once. And no asthma attack either. He actually had fun talking about Griz.

Over the weekend the temperatures dropped below zero, and on Sunday night it snowed six inches. It was still snowing on Monday, but during lunch, the sun came out and the snow slipped out of the valley. Everyone else got to go outside after lunch, but Isaiah's fifth-period teacher made him stay in because of his asthma. He got a pass to the library where he could watch for George. He got there just as George slipped into the cottonwoods.

"He's in," Rose whispered beside him.

"Hi! What are you doing here?" Isaiah was delighted to see her, today in all purple hair and nails.

"I heard you ask for a pass to the library, so I got one to get a new book. I wanted to come and watch George with you."

Isaiah nodded, feeling happy inside.

"This is taking forever!" Rose said sitting down at his table. "I wanted the agency to swoop in and bust the crap out of them! But the realistic part of me knew it would take awhile. I'm scared that they won't do anything because we're a bunch of kids." The librarian looked over at them. Rose lowered her voice. "I couldn't find the dog this weekend. I hope she found somewhere warm to be. I worry about her."

"Do you think her puppies are still with her?"

"I don't know. I've tried to follow her, but I haven't seen any. I'll look for her again after school. After all, I was rescued from a crib in China, so I owe it to her to rescue her from hunger."

Isaiah thought about Rose lying in that crib in China. A tiny baby with no parents. All alone. He sighed deeply.

As if sensing his thoughts, Rose changed the subject. "I overnighted the evidence on Wednesday so they got it on Thursday. They had two days to look at it—and the weekend if they worked then. My parents work all weekend every weekend so I was kind of hoping they do too." The librarian cleared her throat.

"It's hard to wait," Isaiah whispered back.

"Yeah, I hate waiting." Rose got up. "I'd better find a book while George does his thing."

As she moved away, Isaiah sat there pondering. What if the agency didn't listen? What if they thought it was a prank? What if nothing happened? He felt a warmth across his back and down his arms. He heard a message in his head, "We have this and are working from our end." Then he felt Grizzly's breath against his neck.

Right then, George came out of the trees. The ribbon was still there. Isaiah looked at Rose and shrugged.

The rest of the week the ribbon shone on the branch, gently gliding in the breeze. George's watch came to an end. No trouble brewin' yet. Rose kept putting out food for the dog, but there were no sightings of her. Isaiah kept thinking about the Labrador and her puppies. The second week since their first dream together came to a close.

On Sunday, George called again. His mother handed over the phone. "I think it could be that George who called before," she said.

Of course it was. It's not like anyone else ever called him.

"Hey, Isaiah, how are you?" George sounded excited.

"Good." His mother was standing right there listening. Didn't she have something better to do?

"Hey, I wondered if you have Rose's phone number. I need to tell her where I've hidden the binoculars since she starts watch tomorrow."

"No, I don't have it. Sorry."

"Well, I guess it can wait until Monday. Hey! I almost forgot. I get to stay in class all this next week. I'm on trial. My case manager can't believe it, but I'm staying up with the work so I get to try a whole week without her help."

"That's great, George! I am really happy for you!"

"George," his mother said. "I thought so." Now that she knew for sure was she going to leave him alone to have his phone call in privacy? No, apparently not. She acted like she was rearranging the things on the buffet.

"Octopus has really helped me to have confidence in myself," he said. "And so has Rose. I really miss her on the weekends if you know what I mean."

"Uh huh." He didn't, but he thought about the ways Grizzly helped him.

"Hey! The water results should come back this next week."

"You're right. Cool," Isaiah said.

"Well, thanks. See you tomorrow."

"George who?" his mother asked as soon as Isaiah hung up the phone.

"A kid in my class," Isaiah headed back to the living room and their card game.

"What did he want?" his mother asked behind him.

"He wanted a phone number for a girl in our class, but I don't have it."

"Oh! So boys calling girls is starting already," his mother said. "I'm glad you aren't doing that yet."

"Whose deal is it?" Isaiah asked quickly, wanting to distract her from the boys and girls topic.

"Mine," she said. "We're going to have the talk about sex someday soon." Klick. Klack. went her teeth.

Oh no! Quick! "Mom, I'm not ready for that yet. Puberty is taking all of my energy."

She looked at him a long time. She nodded. "Do you have any questions?"

"No. I'll let you know if I do."

"Okay. I want you to get accurate, medical information and not from some back alley somewhere." She began shuffling the cards.

He didn't know why he'd go looking for information in an alley when he could just Google it.

"Raise your hand if you remember the water testing we did a few weeks ago?" was our science teacher's opening question. "Good. Good," he said looking around the room. "The results are back from the water sample George collected. Can I get a drum roll?"

The sound of desks being beaten filled the room. A scientific bar graph sprang onto the screen. Isaiah realized he was holding his breath. He let it out slowly and stole a glance at Rose. She was scrunched way down in her seat. George and Magda were both focused on the screen as their teacher explained how to read the chart. He used terms Isaiah wasn't familiar with, but he could tell from the teacher's tone of voice that the results were a cause for concern. The teacher turned to George, "It's imperative that we notify the state about this immediately. The contents of this pond are extremely toxic. Do you remember exactly where the pond is?"

George nodded, glancing at Rose who now had her head down on her desk.

Isaiah found himself speaking. He hadn't raised his hand, so it took the teacher a moment to identify who was speaking. "I know George is the one who discovered this pond; however, I would like to suggest that the complaint be filed by our whole class. It would be a good learning experience."

The teacher stared at him. Isaiah's voice had sounded deeper inside of him, and there had been no croaks.

"I agree with Isaiah," Magda said. "We should write a letter and all of us should sign it. And you too," she said to the teacher. "If this is okay with George."

"I think it's a great idea," he said, smiling at Isaiah and then at Magda. Isaiah noticed there were no under the breath comments coming from the back of the room.

"I'll write the letter," Rose volunteered. "If it's okay with you," she said to George. "I'll just say one of us in the class found the sample in a pond in town. Then I'll say where it is." Rose quickly arranged her neon orange hair around her ears.

"That's perfect, Rose," George said.

Their science teacher launched into the effects of these toxins on fish, plants, animals and humans. Rose took notes, her orange nails flying.

Isaiah sat back, relieved that George wouldn't have to stand alone, and that Rose seemed appeased. He was also excited that more evidence was headed to join the log book. Now the agency would have their teacher as a contact.

"That was quick thinking, Isaiah," Rose said to him after class. "And don't worry. I've got the letter handled." She hurried away to walk to language arts behind George.

The third day of Rose's watch, the ribbon was gone. Isaiah saw her come out of the trees and look up at the branch. It was obvious to him that she wasn't the one who had removed it. She slipped back into the trees.

He waited just a minute and then followed her. George came next and then Magda.

"What's happening?" Isaiah asked when everyone was there.

"I don't know. It was there when I went in to check on things. It was gone when I came back."

"Is everything the same?" Magda asked.

"No change," Rose reported.

George had his back to them, peeking out onto the school ground. "I see it," he said. "One of the eighth graders has it in her hair."

"Great. Now what?" Rose asked.

"We need to use something natural that won't attract other kids," Magda said.

"What about if we have the signal inside the school?" Rose suggested.

George said, "I have a pen that lights up. The person on watch can turn it on in social science if there's a change."

The kids agreed on this signal. "Pen's not on and nothing's brewin'. It goes on, something's doin'," Rose chanted.

One by one they returned to the school ground.

Chapter 24

Legacy

The pen wasn't lit up on Thursday. The pen wasn't lit up on Friday. Everyone in the science class signed the letter Rose wrote to the agency, and it got mailed with the test results. As he signed it, Isaiah asked Grizzly to do what he could to hurry the response. The weekend came. The weekend went, and Isaiah was on duty. It was also Halloween week. And the temperatures were scheduled to plummet.

On Monday, after quickly eating, Isaiah bundled up and slipped through the trees. He found the binoculars in the white plastic bag beside the rock just as Rose had promised.

The pond was frozen over. Maybe the weather had changed the men's plans. Maybe the ground was too frozen to plow the pond under and hide the evidence of dumping toxins. Staying within the trees, he followed the frozen stream to the gate. He listened to the silence, his breathing even. His glove tried to stick to the gate when he opened it, and the binoculars made cold rings around his eyes right before they fogged over. He wiped them and tried again, but they were too cold. He breathed on the lenses heating them up and wiped again. Better. Inside the warehouse yard, nothing seemed to have changed. Nothing had moved. There was no smoke coming up. The barrels were where they'd been the last time he had looked into this yard. He slid the gate shut and returned along the trees.

Grizzly, he thought, *what is taking so long?* He felt the warmth along his neck and realized that his asthma was absent. And George was still with them in all their core classes. And Rose hadn't gotten in trouble for a long time. Other things were changing. He'd keep being patient about this.

He replaced the binoculars and was heading back to the

school yard when he saw movement out of the corner of his eye. He stopped. At first he thought it was a black squirrel struggling through snow that was over its head. It was trying to get to Isaiah. Then he heard it 'yip'. It was a puppy. He scooped it up. It was shaking. He unzipped his parka and put it against his warm body. It licked his chin. Isaiah laughed.

"Who are you, little guy?" he asked, knowing it must be one of the lab puppies. He looked at the trail the pup had cut through the snow. He followed it.

It led to an overhang, a kind of cave in the rocks. Bending down, he felt the pup skim down his chest and out into the cave. Isaiah's eyes followed it. The cave was fairly dark, but he could smell dogs. And something else.

He felt along the ground and came to frozen fur. He scuttled into the cave further. There was the mother, cold. He pulled her toward the light, the little pup following her. Crying. He felt for a heartbeat and couldn't find one. Her eyes were open, her body stiff in death and from the cold. She couldn't have starved because Rose was feeding her. Had she been drinking from the toxic stream?

He crawled back to where she'd been lying, and there they were. Her puppies. He lifted each one and carried it to the opening. Six were dead. One was at the bottom of the pile. A little female whose tail thumped the ground. He lifted her into his parka and her little brother followed, still crying. He stuck them both inside his shirt, buttoning it up and tucking it into his jeans so they wouldn't fall out. He felt their tiny claws scratching his skin.

He put the other puppies back where he had found them and then carried the mother back into the cave. He laid her on her brood. "You saved two of them," he whispered into her ear. "I am glad you came to us." He remembered the day they buried the birds and how she had stood at a distance watching their compassion in action. "I will take good care of these two," he promised, determined but having no idea how.

Tears froze his eyelashes together as he made his way back to school. The puppies were snuggled against him, quiet. He could feel their tiny hearts beating.

He was glad for the down parka which hid the bulges against his thin body. He found Rose. "I found the mother," he said, fresh tears melting the frozen ones and then refreezing.

Rose pulled him around the corner. George was there in no time. And then Magda. Isaiah told the story between sobs, his nose running. Magda patted his jacket and the pups squirmed.

"Give me the puppies," Rose said. "I'm taking them to the vet right now."

"What about school?" Magda asked.

"I have quite a bit of ditching experience," Rose said. "No problem. I have forging my parents' signatures down to an art."

She was such a good artist, Isaiah had no doubt. "But wait," he said. "I promised the mother…"

"I know," Rose said, but we need to be sure they're okay and that the mother's milk wasn't toxic or anything. I'm sure the water's what killed her."

"Don't let the vet keep them," Isaiah said. "We need to keep them. I need to keep them."

"Okay. I'll call everyone tonight."

Isaiah gave each pup a kiss on the head as he handed it to Rose. They watched her walk off the school grounds.

When the phone rang that night, his mother cleared her throat loudly before she announced, "It's a girl."

"Isaiah, the vet ran blood tests, and the puppies are fine. He said they're about six weeks old," Rose said. "I took him to the cave, and you were right. The others are dead. The vet said the mother hasn't been gone that long. I wish I could have found her before…" Rose's voice trailed off as she quietly cried. "I wanted to rescue her so much."

"You did rescue her in a way, Rose," Isaiah said. "Two of her puppies are still here." His voice broke, more tears coming.

He felt his mother's arm around his shoulders, and he leaned into her just like he had as a little kid. He let the tears flow. "What will happen now, Rose?"

"I have them here. They can stay until we decide, but I would really like to keep the little girl. If it's okay with you. I think I'll name her China."

When he hung up, he told his mother the story of finding the mother and the pups, careful to leave out the warehouse details. He was fully expecting her to be upset that he was out in the cold, so he was stunned when she said, "Obviously if you were outside today rescuing puppies, your asthma is getting better. You may be outgrowing it. Perhaps it's time for us to try a dog."

"Really? Oh mom that would be the best thing ever."

His mom laughed. "What would you name this puppy?"

"Bear!" Isaiah said.

"What is it with you and bears?"

"I like bears a lot," he said.

"It must be because of Pathfinder," she said. "When you were tiny you used to beg me to take you on campus so you could hug the leg of that giant sculpture."

"I did?" This was a story she'd never told him before.

"Yes, I think your love of bears started a long time ago."

Isaiah knew then that Grizzly had always been with him.

"So Bear is at Rose's house tonight?"

He nodded.

"After work tomorrow, we will bring him home. You are responsible for taking care of him, training him, and raising him right. The first two years are very important in making him the kind of dog you want for the ten after that," she said.

"Oh thank you so much, mom," he said hugging her again. "I love you."

He went to sleep with his hand on the tiny scratches on his belly and a smile on his face. Bear!

Chapter 25

Halloween

Magda met him at the front door of the school on Tuesday morning, Halloween Day. The thermometer that morning had been seven degrees below zero. "I'm taking watch the rest of this week. It's too cold for you to be outside," she said. Then she was gone in the rush of kids.

After he stuffed his hat, scarf and gloves into his coat sleeve and hung it up in his locker, he went to first period and placed George's pen on her desk.

He looked down at his Halloween costume with excitement. For years his mother had insisted on him being a clown and had put together mismatched and colorful clothing with the same yarn wig and red, rubber nose. This year he had convinced her that he wanted to be a bear. "You're growing up so I guess that's okay," she'd said. This discussion had taken place before Bear the Labrador puppy and now tonight he was going to pick up him up. He was so excited!

His mother had purchased brown furry material to make the bear suit. He had glued some fur onto one of his baseball caps to form ears and a head and then found a bear nose to wear. He felt very close to Grizzly dressed like this.

"Wow, Griz!" an octopus said to him in a voice that sounded like a muffled George. "You look great!"

"So do you!" George had a full octopus outfit that came down over his whole body. Only his legs from the knees down showed. "Where did you find that costume?"

"It was online at a marine biology site," he said. "It's cool, but I'm really hot in here." There was a muffled laugh. "Is Magda a black panther?"

Isaiah looked around the room and found her. "Yes, she looks great too. She's over there." He had to help George turn because his rubbery legs kept catching on the desks.

"Where's Rose?" he asked.

"I don't see any giraffes," Isaiah said, and then his breath caught. Across the room there was a barrel with a skull and crossbones painted on it. Sticking out of the top of the barrel was lime green hair. Rose! What was she doing? "Oh no," he said to George, turning him toward the barrel of toxins.

"Oh boy… I hope this doesn't come back to hurt us later."

Rose saw the boys looking at her. She signaled with her index finger for them to wait. She turned around. There was a large white sign hanging off of the back of her barrel. In big letters she had painted: Do Something NOW!

She worked her way over to the boys. "It's my statement," she said. Isaiah understood her impatience and how Rose needed to be in-your-face. "Hey! My mom said I can keep the boy puppy. Can we come get him tonight at 5:30?"

"So China's mine?" The barrel of toxins tried to hug the bear. "Yes. Oh yes!"

Before they could explain to George, their math teacher (dressed as Merlin the Magician) called the class together. "Your costumes are wonderful." Everyone clapped. But we're still having classes. The Halloween dance isn't until seventh and eighth periods." Everyone groaned.

Seventh period, Isaiah-Grizzly was bobbing for apples when some rubber octopus legs hit across the back of his knees. Lifting his head, he saw that someone had pushed George. It was one of the mean kids, and it had been on purpose. Isaiah rose, a deep growl rising in his chest. He moved to defend his friend.

"Since when do they make costumes for fat people?" The mean kid was sneering. "And who invited a retard to this party anyway?" He pushed George again, moving him very close to the tank full of water and bouncing apples. "No one wants you here. Go away!" He gave a shove that would have definitely put

George into the water except for Rose, who pushed Isaiah out of the way, and caught him. Isaiah didn't see where she had come from.

"Hey!" she said stepping between them. "Look at the toxic waste that slithered out of my barrel." She was right in the mean kid's face, her hands going for his neck.

George stepped between Rose and the mean kid. In a muffled voice he said, "Rose, thank you. Let's plant some kindness seeds in his garden." He stepped closer to the mean kid and said, "I know you really are a good person inside."

The mean kid stared at George-Octopus. He looked at Rose. He looked at Isaiah. He looked back at George who added, "I know you really can do better."

The mean kid shook his head like the words were mosquitoes surrounding him, biting into his flesh. He scratched his ears. The crowd was growing around them. "Whatever," he finally said as he gave George one final push. Isaiah thought it was more for effect than anything because George's rubber legs didn't even jiggle.

George whispered, "Thank you!" to both of them as he went in the opposite direction of the mean kid.

Before Rose moved, she said, "Wow. He had that all by himself."

Later Isaiah congratulated George on how he handled things with the mean kid.

George said, "I'm still shaking, but I learned I'm brave enough to stand up for myself. That's very cool."

After the games were done and cupcakes and cider had been served, they were moved into the cafeteria. Orange and black lights flashed in time with the loud music. Isaiah stood against the wall watching the dancers. He thought, *if there ever existed a more perfect dance partner for a barrel of toxic wastes, it's an octopus with rubber legs.* Rose's signs were swaying and George's many legs were bouncing up and down. The look on Rose's face was so tender. He wondered if George could see it through his mask.

"Would Griz do Panther the honor?" he heard Magda say beside him.

Magda the Popular wanted to dance with him he thought as Griz gave her his arm and led her onto the floor with a flourish. A flourish only a very confident bear could have. At once he was grateful to his mother for making him dance with her at weddings. He knew what to do and as Griz, he was quite graceful.

The song ended, and Magda made no moves to leave. "Let's keep dancing," she said.

He bowed.

The next song was slow. He looked at her to see if she still wanted to dance with him. She came toward him, and he embraced her in a bear hug. As the panther and the bear moved to the music in the flashing Halloween light, Isaiah realized that he never wanted this song to end.

When the party ended, Magda said, "We're both leaders so it just makes sense. See you tomorrow." And she was gone, her soccer bag flying behind her with her tail.

This left Isaiah with a lot to think about beginning with the fact that she saw him as a leader and ending with the dread that she might start calling him, unleashing his mother's Klick. Klack. Accurate. Medical. Talk. About. Sex. The dog had distracted her from Rose's phone call, but if Magda started calling... oh boy... But tonight Bear the Pup was his. He filled up with happiness about that instead.

"Okay, time for you two to go to bed," his mother said that night at 9:30. She didn't believe in trick or treating past elementary school, so he and Bear had kept busy all night handing out Halloween candy. Bear hadn't minded the ghosts and witches and robots and Grim Reaper's who had wanted to pet him. He loved his new house and had sniffed everywhere at least twice. He was really smart too and knew just what to do when Isaiah put him outside in the snow. They laid newspapers in the kitchen though, just in case.

"Bed," he said to Bear, patting his mattress, but the pup was still too small to jump up.

His mom scooped him up and tucked him in under Isaiah's arm. "My two sweet boys," she said. She kissed each of them good night and turned off the lamp.

"Mom," Isaiah said, "thanks again. I will take good care of Bear."

"I know you will," she said as she closed his door.

"I promised your mom the same thing," he said to Bear, his voice catching as he remembered her frozen body on top of her pups. Bear gave a little whimper as he snuggled closer to Isaiah.

Chapter 26

Volcano

Magda hadn't called on Halloween night, but she did hand him a note at his locker first thing the next morning. "Since you don't text," she said before disappearing panther-like.

The note read: *Rose is such a hypocrite. She makes this huge deal about not getting busted for you-know-what, and then she shows up in that costume. I can't believe her!*

November first. Already. Isaiah wondered if time was going fast because he had friends this year or if this was the part about growing up where adults always said, "It will be over before you know it." He pondered what he would write back to Magda, not really sure what to say.

After first period, she asked, "Did you write me?"

"Not yet," he said.

And so it went after second period. He had no note to hand her because he still didn't know what to say.

In language arts, they got their grades for the PowerPoint— an A. The teacher had written, "Excellent demonstration of cause and effect."

"We're masters of that for sure," Rose commented which gave Isaiah what he needed. At the end of class, he handed Magda a note, *"It's all about cause and effect. Wait and see what happens next."*

"You're very deep," she said. And then she was gone. And he had more to ponder.

Coming out of the library after lunch, Isaiah saw a crowd gathered in front of the girls' bathroom. Magda and Rose were in the middle. Magda's face was red, and she had a hold on Rose's arm.

Rose, whose hair was lemon yellow today, looked at Magda and said, "Remember Volcano. Either destroy or change. I'm choosing change."

Magda let out a loud "Urg!" and then she stomped off.

"Volcano?" Isaiah heard one kid say. "They were fighting over a volcano? Weird."

Isaiah was amazed by the change in Rose. She was so calm. He tried to catch her eye, but she just pushed past everyone on her way to class. Her face was closed like it had been after she talked about the Chinese orphanage.

He tried to find Magda, but she had disappeared. He wrote his second note to her, *"What happened? Are you okay?"* He dropped it through the slits in her locker.

Chapter 27

The Leak

That night George called Isaiah. This time his mother nodded and left the room saying, "I'm glad you have a little friend."

Seriously? he thought. "Hey, what's up?" he asked George. "Have you talked to Rose?"

"Yeah, I went over to see her and China after school because (drum roll) I'm officially off grounding. Anyway, she's okay. Just hurt that Magda called her a hypocrite. And proud of herself for not punching Magda. Personally I'm more proud of her for not strangling the mean kid at the party." They laughed.

In a hushed voice, George continued. "I think we're all tired of waiting for the state to respond. I get why Rose wore the barrel for Halloween. I get her frustration. It's taking forever. So I kind of leaked the story to my sister."

"What?" Isaiah shouted. His mother came around the corner with a look of concern on her face. So she hadn't gone far.

"I told her that I heard a rumor about toxic waste at the warehouse. She has to keep where she heard the rumor a secret. Protect her sources is what she called it. So she'll tell her friends who work at the radio station, and they'll follow up on it."

Isaiah let his breath out. He hadn't realized he was holding it in. He gave his mother a 'go away' look. She let out a sigh and returned to the living room. He picked up Bear who was playing tug with the bottom of Isaiah's jeans.

"So anyway, she's going to have her friends do some journalistic research. Make some calls to be sure the agency is on it."

"Can they trace it back to you?" Isaiah asked, stepping into the kitchen and covering the mouthpiece with his hand. "After all, the whole science class knows you're the one who found the pond water."

"No, her friends will be calling as representatives of the radio station. She's going to suggest they do a follow-up piece on the new business and how it's going. It'll be okay," George assured him.

"Have you told Rose?" Isaiah asked.

"No, I will tomorrow, but I don't think I'll be the one to tell Magda. I thought it was Rose who was so worried about being linked to this whole thing. Now it seems like it's Magda."

"I'll tell her," Isaiah said, dreading that discussion already.

"Okay," George said and then he added, "Isaiah, you aren't mad at me for doing this are you?"

"No, it was on our list of possibilities. It's going at it from several different angles kind of forcing them to act." George sighed. Isaiah added, "It's a stroke of genius really."

George sounded like he was smiling when he said thanks.

"What was he thinking?" Magda stormed at Isaiah the next morning. "Things are getting out of control. This could hurt my chances at a soccer scholarship!"

"That's a few years off, Magda," Isaiah said trying to calm her down, wondering why she couldn't see that she was the one getting out of control. Now he understood more about why she was upset. Her successful soccer future. She had something big to lose. "No one remembers that Rose was toxic waste, and it's George's sisters' friends. You haven't been tied to any of it. And now maybe we'll know something soon."

"Well, I'm not happy with any of you right now." She stomped away.

No calls. No notes. No secret glances. It was just like old times, and Isaiah didn't like it one bit. And he didn't know why she was mad at him. What had he done?

Then on Friday, when they got to social sciences, the pen was lit. Magda seemed to be shaking as she took notes with it; the light bouncing with each dotted 'i' and crossed 't'.

Isaiah's heart raced, wondering what had happened. What had she seen?

They gathered by Isaiah's locker after class. Magda had just enough time to report, "There's yellow caution tape all the way around the pond and big toxic contaminate signs everywhere along the warehouse fence. They have the whole area closed off. Something's doin'."

Saturday morning, Isaiah was gaming while Bear ran at the sounds coming out of the TV. It was so funny to watch the pup trying to catch something he couldn't see.

The phone rang, and it was Magda. He caught it before his mother could. When she picked up the extension, he said, "I have it, mom." He waited for the click before he continued. "Okay," he said. "Hi."

"I apologize for the way I've been acting," Magda started the conversation. "I've never had friends like all of you before. Usually I'm in charge of everything that happens in my group so there are no surprises. I'm definitely not big on surprises. You're all so different from what I'm used to, and it was kind of freaking me out. Especially Rose. She scares me in a way. But I've been thinking about it, and I was miserable on Thursday. I was so happy I had something to report yesterday so you'd all speak to me again. I was a brat. Sorry."

"That's okay," Isaiah said, searching for words. "I understand."

"Good. I don't want you to think I'm weird. I'm glad we don't have to keep watch at lunch anymore. Maybe we can eat together sometimes." She hung up.

This puberty-girls stuff was more confusing than anything. He really didn't understand.

The warehouse follow-up story ran on the college radio station the following Tuesday, four weeks to the day the kids had reported it to the agency.

Isaiah listened to the program before his mom got home from

work that evening. He and Bear were sitting on the couch, and Isaiah was stroking the silky-smooth inside of the pup's ears. His training book said to regularly touch the dog's ears and paws to build trust.

The radio station had been unable to get any comments from the agency other than they had received some tips and were following up on them, but the reporter noted that the warehouse appeared to have been abandoned and that there were barrels full of toxic waste in the back of it. She had alerted the local authorities.

As he pulled one long ear through his fingers, he said, "You know, Bear, I feel really happy that the steps we've taken are getting some results. That's called cause-effect, you know." The pup sniffed at his fingers. "But I'm also kind of sad. It's like we've all worked together on this secret project and now that it's done, I feel sad." Bear looked at him and then jumped up and licked his face.

Chapter 28

Invitation

"We're going to have Thanksgiving dinner with the Duncan family this year," his mother said Thursday night at dinner. "Apparently you and Magda are friends, and she asked her mother to invite us." His mother's voice ended more like she was asking a question.

Usually his mother made all of his favorite dishes for Thanksgiving: broccoli cheese casserole, her special angel salad with whipped cream, pumpkin pie, and of course, turkey and mashed potatoes. "Will you be bringing your angel salad and the broccoli casserole?" he asked, trying to hide his surprise and avoid any discussion about Magda.

"Yes. Now tell me why I didn't know about you and Magda."

"It's no big deal, mom. We did a project together in language arts, and we became friends, I guess."

She stared at him a long time. Her teeth were quiet. No Klick. Klack. "Okay," she said. "Bear is also invited to come along."

"Tell me one of your sorority stories," he said. His mother and Marci, Magda's mom, had been in the same sorority at the university. He knew they were old college friends, but he didn't know they talked to each other anymore. Great.

His mother launched a story he'd heard before about exchanging furniture in their sorority house, carrying heavy couches up and down stairs, to see if anyone noticed the change. Isaiah thought it was interesting she had picked a story about change. More cause and effect. The theme of seventh grade so far. Thanksgiving was two weeks from today. He'd better ask Grizzly for some advice.

On Friday, all Magda had to say was, "I'm glad you're coming over for Thanksgiving. It just makes sense." Again, Isaiah wasn't sure how.

Every day he and Rose compared notes on China and Bear whenever they thought of something cute to share with each other. She always had pictures on her phone to show him too. He wished he had a camera so he could document Bear.

Friday night he asked his mother if they had a camera around the house. She said, "An old Pentax that takes real film. I don't know where you'd buy film. Sorry."

So he began doing sketches of Bear. Maybe it was the subject, but he loved to draw. He spent Saturday morning drawing Bear instead of gaming, and he made one big drawing of Griz. He pinned that next to his bed. *Maybe this will help me remember my dreams again,* he thought.

George called Sunday evening to tell him that he'd taken Rose ice skating. "I just might have some athletic ability after all," he announced. "I didn't fall once. Of course she was holding my hand the whole time." Isaiah wondered what it might be like to take Magda skating, and he wondered what it might be like to hold her hand. He shut the thought off just in case his mother beamed into his vibes and started klacking.

Snow seemed to be falling every other day, and it was cold. Despite that, Bear was progressing nicely with his training. He sure loved that little guy who seemed to grow every day. And his asthma didn't act up at all—with the cold or with the dog. Maybe he had outgrown it.

Magda stopped asking if he had a note for her and was still to hanging out with her old friends at lunch.

They all hoped that clean-up had begun at the warehouse even though it was cold and snowing.

On Thursday, a week before Thanksgiving, their science teacher announced that they had a special guest today. A woman was sitting on a high stool in the corner, her gray hair in a big bun on top of her head and a pair of black-framed glasses pushed neatly into the arrangement. She was from the agency they had sent their letter to. Isaiah's heart began to flutter with a little anxiety and lots of excitement. Someone had actually come up all the way from Denver to talk to them.

After being introduced, she scooted her chair into the center of the room, cleared her throat, and said, "I want to thank all of you for notifying our agency about the toxins in the water. We appreciated your letter and are grateful that there are young people in our state who are concerned about the environment. That is very encouraging. We also received a telephone tip about a warehouse here in town where toxic substances were spotted. Our caller didn't give a name, but we think she could have also been a young person from this school. This person mailed us a detailed log book and photographs that were extremely helpful to our investigators. We are so grateful because this information led us to the warehouse which was the source of the pollution in the pond. If that anonymous caller is in this room, thank you from the State of Colorado." It seemed as if she looked right at Magda.

Magda said, "It wasn't me, but as a citizen of this state, I am grateful too." She looked around the room.

Isaiah hoped she hadn't given herself away while she was trying to cover her involvement. He raised his hand. "Can you tell us what is being done to clean up the area?"

The woman put on her glasses and began reading and explaining the action plan she was holding. As he listened, he realized that while they knew there were impacts to everything in the area, they'd really had no idea how far reaching they were. And what was involved in cleaning it all up. And how many years some of those poisons could affect the land and the water. He was aware that his mouth was hanging open in amazement, and he quickly shut it. His stomach felt tight as she talked about the impact on animals. He was certain that drinking the water is what had killed Bear's mother. And he was so glad that they hadn't touched the bird pellets. The woman explained how that poison could hurt someone just by getting it on their skin. "Are there any questions?"

There were, but none from George, Rose, Magda or Isaiah. They high-fived each other with their eyes.

Before she left, the woman said, "If the person or persons from the phone trip are in this room, thank you. We'd love to know who you are so we can thank you personally. Someone also gave a tip to the college radio station which ran an investigation of their own. The story aired last week, and if you didn't get a chance to hear it, you might want to check their archives for it."

Isaiah called a meeting for lunch. It was too cold to go outside, so they met at a back table in the library.

"Do you think I gave myself away?" Magda asked.

Rose responded, "It probably would have been better not to say anything, but I don't think it's a big deal. George, I think you deserve a big thank you for your log book." She smiled at him.

"And for closing the valve," said Isaiah.

"I think we owe a lot to Jeremiah for helping us with that plan," George said. "And Wind and Fire and our power animals. And Magda for making the call. And Rose for almost getting caught by a madman." They all laughed.

"I'm sorry for getting mad at all of you, especially you, Rose." Magda tugged on her ponytail.

"It's okay. We all had our moments, but in the end, we were successful AND none of us got in trouble. That's something new for me." Rose smiled at all of them. "And I have China, and Isaiah has Bear."

"I miss our dreams," Isaiah said with a long sigh.

"Yeah," they said in unison. And the bell rang.

Chapter 29

Flow

Friday was a little warmer so many kids went outside after lunch. Isaiah went back to the library. He found a comfortable chair and opened a book in his lap so he looked like he was reading. He pulled his hoodie over his head and closed his eyes. *Grizzly, can you explain relationships with girls to me? Or more specifically my relationship with Magda?*

He was in the meadow, Griz beside him. They walked to a blue, sparkling lake. The water was so clear Isaiah could see rainbow-colored fish flashing past. Grizzly dove in and signaled Isaiah to follow. Isaiah dove in and warm and soothing water flowed around him as he began swimming. He followed Grizzly to a river that was flowing out of the lake. When Isaiah took breaths, the air tasted fresh, almost crispy. "Thank you, Wind!" he thought. Grizzly flipped onto his back and launched himself head first down the river. At a little waterfall, Isaiah watched Grizzly's feet disappear over the edge. Isaiah followed. The waterfall sounded like it was giggling as he floated over it. He was airborne for a minute and then he felt watery fingers gently floating his head on top of the water. He sank into the river as it guided him around rocks and past log jams. It must be a magic river, he thought. He closed his eyes, letting the water massage him.

Grizzly pulled him out at a bend in the river and placed Isaiah up on his back. Grizzly's fur was warm as Isaiah buried his face in it. Hot air dried his hair and clothes as they flew back to the meadow.

He knew he had received the answer to his question. But what did it mean?

Back in his chair in the library, Isaiah thought about the journey's message. The river must represent his relationship with Magda. Relationship River? He dove in, swam, went head first down the river and it all worked out okay. He was supported and when he let the flow carry him, he didn't hit any rocks or get in any log jams. Okay. The bell rang.

On Saturday morning, he did some more sketches. Then he laid them all side by side along one wall. Bear ran happily over them, sniffing each one. He finally sat down on the picture of Bear sitting beside Pathfinder, the statue at the college which Isaiah had drawn from memory. "Would you like to meet Pathfinder someday?" he asked Bear. The puppy yipped.

His mom came into the den. She saw the sketches and stopped to admire each of them. "You really have a talent for drawing," she said to him.

"Thanks. I am drawing him since we don't have a camera."

"They are very good," she said. "Speaking of cameras, I've been thinking about Christmas. Would you like Santa to bring you a phone?"

"YES!"

His mother laughed. "I've been looking at family plans. Perhaps this afternoon we should go shopping?"

Bear's tail was wagging hard, and his 'yip' sounded just like "yes"!

On Sunday he took hundreds of pictures and video of Bear which he couldn't wait to share with his friends. He also sent his dad a text message with his new phone number. His dad sent a text back saying he would call on Thanksgiving night. "Can't wait to hear about this new girlfriend of yours." *Oh boy…*

They only had two days of school because of Thanksgiving. Magda was thrilled about his phone and taught him how to set up a calendar which he doubted he'd need. She put Thanksgiving Dinner on it with an emoji of a heart next to it.

Isaiah imagined he was floating on the river again going head first over a waterfall. At least he knew he wouldn't drown.

Chapter 30

Thanksgiving

"My name's Robb," the big man said to Isaiah's mom as he stuck his hand out. "I don't know if you remember me. Chemistry 201. Sophomore year at the U."

His mom said, "Yes, I remember the fire you started in a lab."

Robb let out a loud laugh. "Not one of my better days. And who's this?"

"I'm Isaiah." He shook the big hand. A heavy gold ring with several diamonds ground into his finger. Robb had a lot of hair sticking out of his shirt below his neck. He smelled like beer.

"So this is Isaiah." Robb said it in a high-pitch, sing-song voice and then he laughed loudly again. "Magda's little boyfriend." The way he said boyfriend sounded like it had five syllables.

His mother ground her nails into Isaiah's shoulder as she guided him through the Duncan's living room which was filled with the smells of dinner. "Marci," she called. "Is there anything you need help with?"

Magda came up from the basement. "All the kids are down here," she said to Isaiah. "Come on, Bear." The pup gingerly hopped down stairs that were almost as tall as he was.

As Isaiah turned to follow, his mother bent down and whispered in his ear, "Don't worry about Robb. He's always been an ass. Now go have fun."

Isaiah had rarely ever heard his mother swear. *Lots of surprises come with puberty*, he thought.

At dinner, they were all seated around the same table—adults and kids. While Magda's dad carved the turkey, Robb said, "Good looking bird. Plump. Ready to be devoured. I'll take as much flesh as you can give me." He stuck his plate out.

Isaiah suddenly did not want to eat the turkey. He remembered the beautiful blackbird that had died at his feet. One last breath. Gone.

Robb continued, "Did I tell you that last year I shot the turkey for my Thanksgiving dinner?" He went on to describe, in detail, the hunt. Isaiah felt tears constricting his throat.

Magda said, "Uncle Robb, not everyone likes to hear hunting stories."

Isaiah smiled at her, wondering if she was remembering too.

Uncle Robb said, "Only anti-hunting hippies and those people in Boulder. Everyone else knows animals are here to serve man." He took a swig from a long, brown beer bottle.

Isaiah felt Bear snuggle between his feet, and he thought about the frozen, lifeless body of Bear's mother protecting her pups even in death.

"So Robb, where are you living now?" his mother asked.

"Kansas City. I run a large corporation. Make investments. Actually I make lots of money." He laughed again. "At least I usually do. Just suffered a big loss due to stupid EPA rules. Here in town as a matter of fact."

"So you're the one," Isaiah said, facing the man. He felt Grizzly power fill him.

"Yes, I'm the bad guy that killed a couple of fish," Robb said. "Everyone got their shorts in a knot over it." He laughed loudly.

"You killed more than a few fish," Isaiah felt himself growing bigger. "You also killed 109 birds and a mother Labrador and six of her puppies. And that's what we know about."

"Son, it's just business. You'll understand when you're older." Robb drank some more beer.

Isaiah could not believe what he was hearing. "I understand now," he growled. "It's called cause and effect. You made choices that have had a big impact on a lot of things in the environment. I hope you'll learn to make better choices in the future."

Robb laughed again. "That's cute. I guess if they slap me with enough fines. Pass the potatoes." He scooped a big pile onto his plate.

Isaiah said very clearly, "Businesses are run by people who determine their level of integrity." Bear licked his leg under his jeans, and then he felt a foot on his other leg. Magda met his eyes, and he knew he'd gone around the bend in the river.

Robb snorted. "Good luck with that. Integrity and business don't go hand in hand." He turned to Magda's dad. "So I can't wait to hit the slopes tomorrow. Is there anything new since the last time I was here?"

After helping with dishes, Isaiah and Magda went downstairs to watch a movie with her siblings. She sent him a text, "I was so proud of you. You really stood up to Uncle Robb."

Isaiah wrote back, "I was proud that two of the people who got him shut down were sitting at that table! Integrity scored!"

She took his hand and pulled a pillow over it so the kids wouldn't see. He squeezed her hand and sighed. This wasn't hard. He let the river carry him.

As he and his mother were leaving, Uncle Robb pulled Isaiah aside. "Son, your passion is admirable. It's rare in someone so young. It's too late for this old codger to change, but you keep it up. There's a place for you."

"People can always change," Isaiah said. "It's never too late."

"Guess I'll have to give that some thought," he said. He pounded on Isaiah's back. Hard. "Take good care of my niece!"

In the car his mother said, "That man is insufferable." She sighed. "I was proud of the way you stood up to him at dinner. You're really growing up."

Isaiah smiled. *I've got this,* he thought.

She went on, "I'm ready to hear the rest of the story about Robb's warehouse, and your part in getting it shut down." *So she already knew he'd been involved.*

Isaiah told her everything.

Chapter 31

Upper World

On Saturday the four of them went ice skating. While they laced up their skates, Magda told the story of Thanksgiving dinner. "Isaiah said the owner's of businesses determine the integrity the business has, i.e.: you don't have any, Uncle Robb. It was beautiful." She laughed.

"That took major courage," Rose said.

"Standing up to bullies is an art form," George said, fist tapping Isaiah's.

"Especially when you're in an octopus costume," Isaiah said. "That's the real art form."

They moved out onto the ice.

"Hooray for us!" Rose shouted. She linked arms with Magda, chanting, "Octo-Gira-Bear and Pant. We no longer need to rant."

"We know there's nothing that we can't," Magda added, looking at Isaiah as she linked her other arm through his.

"Change our lives in a mo-mant." Isaiah said, hooking arms with George.

"With the help of our power animals, words of kindness we do plant!"George finished. Everyone laughed.

The four of them skated around and around the lake. It was a blue-sky Colorado day. Their breath froze in front of them, but skating with friends kept them warm.

When they took a break, Isaiah took in a deep, deep breath. "It's so great." He fell backwards off the log into a snow bank, pulling George with him.

George, looking up at the sky, said, "I wonder if we'll ever share dreams again?"

"Well, we haven't tried journeying to Upper World yet," Rose said, making a snow angel.

"Let's go there now," Magda said, lying down in the snow beside Isaiah.

"The landscape is different from Lower World," George commented. "Airy, misty maybe."

"I'll meet you on a cloud then," Isaiah said. "Let's tour Upper World." He put his arm over his eyes.

Eagle flew overhead and called to them. He circled, lifted his wings, and flew into the sun. The kids followed.

About the Authors

Sandra Ingerman, MA, is an award winning author of ten books, including *Soul Retrieval: Mending the Fragmented Self, Medicine for the Earth: How to Heal Personal and Environmental Toxins* and *Walking in Light: The Everyday Empowerment of Shamanic Life*. She is the presenter of eight audio programs produced by Sounds True, and she is the creator of the Transmutation App. Sandra is a world renowned teacher of shamanism and has been teaching for more than 30 years. She has taught workshops internationally on shamanic journeying, healing, and reversing environmental pollution using spiritual methods. Sandra is recognized for bridging ancient cross-cultural healing methods into our modern culture addressing the needs of our times.

Sandra is devoted to teaching people how we can work together as a global community to bring about positive change for the planet. She is passionate about helping people to reconnect with nature.

Sandra is a licensed marriage and family therapist and professional mental health counselor. She is also a board-certified expert on traumatic stress. She was awarded the 2007 Peace Award from the Global Foundation for Integrative Medicine. Sandra was chosen as one of the Top 10 Spiritual Leaders of 2013 by Spirituality and Health Magazine.

www.sandraingerman.com

www.shamanicteachers.com

Katherine Wood, MA, taught reading and writing to middle and high school students for 31 years, twelve of those as the Literacy Coordinator for a large metropolitan high school. She has over 2000 hours of shamanic training, teaches shamanic classes and has a shamanic healing practice. She is a member of the Society of Children Book Writers and Illustrators, was a co-creator of

The Colorado Blue Spruce Young Adult Book Award, and has an extensive resume of both taking and teaching writing workshops since the early 1980s. She was the Colorado English Teacher of the Year in 1990.

She has had poetry and professional articles published. This is her first young adult book.

Katherine is an avid reader, writer, and a journeyer who loves to travel both in ordinary reality and in the hidden worlds. She believes that we can bridge these worlds, bringing gifts through to help all of humanity.

www.KatherineWoodAuthor.org

E-Mail: KatherineWoodAuthor@Comcast.net

Moon Books

PAGANISM & SHAMANISM

What is Paganism? A religion, a spirituality, an alternative belief system, nature worship? You can find support for all these definitions (and many more) in dictionaries, encyclopaedias, and text books of religion, but subscribe to any one and the truth will evade you. Above all Paganism is a creative pursuit, an encounter with reality, an exploration of meaning and an expression of the soul. Druids, Heathens, Wiccans and others, all contribute their insights and literary riches to the Pagan tradition. Moon Books invites you to begin or to deepen your own encounter, right here, right now.

If you have enjoyed this book, why not tell other readers by posting a review on your preferred book site. Recent bestsellers from Moon Books are:

Journey to the Dark Goddess
How to Return to Your Soul
Jane Meredith
Discover the powerful secrets of the Dark Goddess and transform your depression, grief and pain into healing and integration.
Paperback: 978-1-84694-677-6 ebook: 978-1-78099-223-5

Shamanic Reiki
Expanded Ways of Working with Universal Life Force Energy
Llyn Roberts, Robert Levy
Shamanism and Reiki are each powerful ways of healing; together,
their power multiplies. Shamanic Reiki introduces techniques to
help healers and Reiki practitioners tap ancient healing wisdom.
Paperback: 978-1-84694-037-8 ebook: 978-1-84694-650-9

Pagan Portals – The Awen Alone
Walking the Path of the Solitary Druid
Joanna van der Hoeven
An introductory guide for the solitary Druid, The Awen Alone
will accompany you as you explore, and seek out your own place
within the natural world.
Paperback: 978-1-78279-547-6 ebook: 978-1-78279-546-9

A Kitchen Witch's World of Magical Herbs & Plants
Rachel Patterson
A journey into the magical world of herbs and plants, filled with
magical uses, folklore, history and practical magic. By popular
writer, blogger and kitchen witch, Tansy Firedragon.
Paperback: 978-1-78279-621-3 ebook: 978-1-78279-620-6

Medicine for the Soul
The Complete Book of Shamanic Healing
Ross Heaven
All you will ever need to know about shamanic healing and how to
become your own shaman…
Paperback: 978-1-78099-419-2 ebook: 978-1-78099-420-8

Shaman Pathways – The Druid Shaman
Exploring the Celtic Otherworld
Danu Forest
A practical guide to Celtic shamanism with exercises and
techniques as well as traditional lore for exploring the Celtic
Otherworld.
Paperback: 978-1-78099-615-8 ebook: 978-1-78099-616-5

Traditional Witchcraft for the Woods and Forests
A Witch's Guide to the Woodland with Guided Meditations and
Pathworking
Melusine Draco
A Witch's guide to walking alone in the woods, with guided
meditations and pathworking.
Paperback: 978-1-84694-803-9 ebook: 978-1-84694-804-6

Wild Earth, Wild Soul
A Manual for an Ecstatic Culture
Bill Pfeiffer
Imagine a nature-based culture so alive and so connected,
spreading like wildfire. This book is the first flame…
Paperback: 978-1-78099-187-0 ebook: 978-1-78099-188-7

Naming the Goddess
Trevor Greenfield
Naming the Goddess is written by over eighty adherents and
scholars of Goddess and Goddess Spirituality.
Paperback: 978-1-78279-476-9 ebook: 978-1-78279-475-2

Shapeshifting into Higher Consciousness
Heal and Transform Yourself and Our World with Ancient
Shamanic and Modern Methods
Llyn Roberts
Ancient and modern methods that you can use every day to
transform yourself and make a positive difference in the world.
Paperback: 978-1-84694-843-5 ebook: 978-1-84694-844-2

Readers of ebooks can buy or view any of these bestsellers by
clicking on the live link in the title. Most titles are published in
paperback and as an ebook. Paperbacks are available in traditional
bookshops. Both print and ebook formats are available online.

Find more titles and sign up to our readers' newsletter at
http://www.johnhuntpublishing.com/paganism
Follow us on Facebook at https://www.facebook.com/MoonBooks
and Twitter at https://twitter.com/MoonBooksJHP